WILLIAM WENTON
AND THE
IMPOSSIBLE
PUZZLE

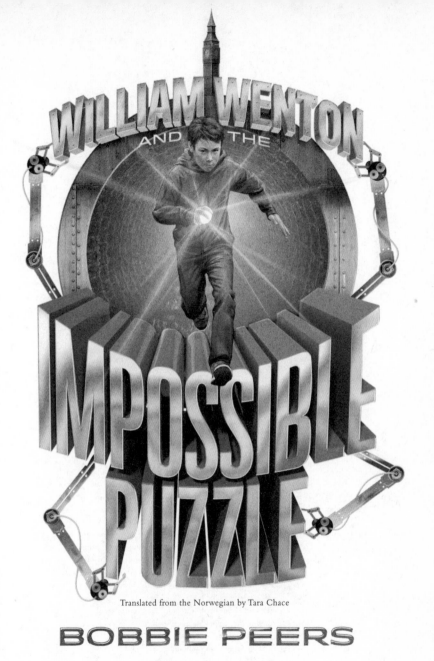

WILLIAM WENTON AND THE IMPOSSIBLE PUZZLE

Translated from the Norwegian by Tara Chace

BOBBIE PEERS

Aladdin

New York London Toronto Sydney New Delhi

ALADDIN

An imprint of Simon & Schuster Children's Publishing Division
1230 Avenue of the Americas, New York, New York 10020
First Aladdin hardcover edition May 2017
Text copyright © 2016 by Bobbie Peers
English language translation copyright © 2017 by Salomonsson Agency
Originally published in 2015 in Norwegian as *Luridiumstyven*
Published by arrangement with Salomonsson Agency
Jacket illustration of type, gears, tunnel, and ivy copyright © 2017 by Luke Lucas
Jacket illustration of boy copyright © 2017 by Eric Deschamps
All rights reserved, including the right of reproduction in whole or in part in any form.
ALADDIN and related logo are registered trademarks of Simon & Schuster, Inc.
For information about special discounts for bulk purchases, please contact Simon & Schuster
Special Sales at 1-866-506-1949 or business@simonandschuster.com.
The Simon & Schuster Speakers Bureau can bring authors to your live event.
For more information or to book an event, contact the Simon & Schuster Speakers Bureau
at 1-866-248-3049 or visit our website at www.simonspeakers.com.
Book designed by Jessica Handelman
The text of this book was set in Bembo.
Manufactured in the United States of America 0417 FFG
2 4 6 8 10 9 7 5 3 1
Library of Congress Control Number 2017934581
ISBN 978-1-4814-7825-0 (hc)
ISBN 978-1-4814-7827-4 (eBook)

To Michelle,
had it not been for you, this book
would never have been!

VICTORIA STATION,
LONDON

It was the middle of morning rush hour. Busy people of every shape and size scurried this way and that. Everyone was minding their own business. No one noticed an elderly man with a beard and round glasses running through the hall. He was clutching a brown parcel and constantly looking behind him, as if he was being chased.

He stumbled on a suitcase someone was wheeling by. It took him a few steps to catch his balance, and then he proceeded down the escalator to the underground trains.

Down on the platform, people were crowded together like lemmings on a cliff. The man pushed his way through the crowd and stopped at the end of the platform. A cool breeze blew out of the tunnel. A train was coming.

None of the other travelers noticed the man jumping

down onto the tracks. The screech of an approaching train could be heard, and the air pressure coming from the tunnel made his long beard flap.

The old man cast one last look at the platform before he turned and disappeared into the dark tunnel.

EIGHT YEARS LATER.
AT A SECRET ADDRESS
SOMEWHERE IN NORWAY.

William was so engrossed in what he was doing that he didn't hear his mother calling him. He sat hunched over a massive desk. With a steady hand he tightened the final screw into a metal cylinder the size of an empty toilet paper roll. The cylinder was divided into several sections that were engraved with various symbols and inscriptions.

William held the cylinder up to the light and studied it with satisfaction. He picked up a newspaper clipping with a picture of a cylinder that looked like the one he was holding in his hand. It said THE IMPOSSIBLE PUZZLE: THE WORLD'S MOST DIFFICULT CODE IS COMING TO NORWAY. CAN YOU BREAK IT?

Even though William had already read the article hundreds of times, he read it again now. He glanced at the picture of the enigmatic metal cylinder. A group of the world's best cryptographers had spent more than three years creating it. And now it was on its introductory tour with the tagline "world's most difficult code." It had the reputation of being impossible to crack. Some of the world's smartest people had already tried—and failed. And now it had finally come to Norway, but after tomorrow night the exhibit would be moving on to Finland, so it was now or never.

"DINNER!" his mother yelled from the kitchen.

William didn't react. In his defense, sound did not travel particularly well in this house. The walls of every room were covered in bookshelves that were jam-packed with books that had been inherited from his grandfather, along with strict instructions never to get rid of them. The books had been hauled over from England in seven big containers. William had read them all. At least twice.

It had been eight years since they'd had to leave England. Eight years since they'd moved into the house. And eight years since Grandfather had disappeared. Now William and his parents lived incognito, at a secret address, with new names, in a narrow country called Norway.

"WILLIAM OLSEN! DINNER!"

His mother didn't let up. William heard her now. She had said Olsen, William Olsen. He was just never going to get used to that name. He longed for the day when he could tell everyone his actual name: William Wenton.

He'd given up asking what really happened back in London eight years earlier. About why they were named Olsen now and had learned Norwegian. About why they lived here, of all places, and about what had happened to Grandfather. His parents had decided not to talk about it. As if all the secrets were better than the truth.

He didn't know much about what had happened, but he did know that it had something to do with a car accident. The same car accident that had left his father paralyzed.

But there was more. Something so serious that their family had to disappear, and a thin little country that almost no one in the rest of the world could find on a map had been the perfect place to disappear to—for as long as it lasted.

"DIIIINNER!!" Mama yelled yet again.

"I just have to fix one little thing first . . . ," William mumbled to himself.

Then it was his father's turn to holler from the distance. "WILLIAM . . . IT'S TIME FOR DINNER!"

William delicately rotated the metal cylinder, feeling how the small pieces rested perfectly in his hands as if they understood him. He jumped when the door to his room suddenly flew open, hitting a tall stack of books and knocking them over. One of the books hit the cylinder, which slipped out of his hands, landed on the floor with a clank and started rolling. William was leaning down to pick it up when his father drove over the threshold in his electric wheelchair, on a collision course with the cylinder. William watched in dismay. A metallic crunch was the only sound as the full weight of one wheel drove over it. His father braked abruptly. The ruined electronics sparked, and a little cloud of smoke rose from the wreckage under the wheel. His father glanced down at his chair in irritation and wrinkled his nose.

"Is it playing up again? I just took it in to get it serviced," he muttered to himself, and then turned his stern eyes to William, who moved his hand to cover the newspaper clipping on the desk.

"It's time for dinner . . . NOW!" said his father before putting his chair in reverse, bumping into another stack of books, and then driving back out of the room.

William waited until the hum of his father's stair lift faded before he stood up. He took a breath. That was close. But his father hadn't seen anything, had he? William was quite sure that he'd managed to hide the newspaper clipping before his father noticed it. He walked over to the cylinder and picked it up. One side was crumpled in. He shook it a little.

"Really?" he said to himself, irritated, and glanced at a thick chain lock on the inside of his door. How had he forgotten to lock it? He always locked his door when he was working on code breaking.

William turned and walked back over to the desk. He

opened one of the drawers and put the newspaper clipping and what was left of the cylinder into it. He stood there for a bit, staring at the other things in the big drawer: a mechanical hand he'd built himself; a 3-D metal puzzle; a completely normal Rubik's Cube; and a shoebox that contained a soldering iron, some small screwdrivers, and a pair of pliers.

He closed the drawer and locked it with a key he hid in a crack between two floorboards. He gave the room a last once-over to make sure he'd stowed everything away.

For some reason or other his father hated cryptography. He'd forbidden any form of code-breaking activity. He wanted William to do the stuff normal children did: soccer, band practice, whatever. It was almost as if his father was afraid of codes and afraid that William would be interested in them. And it was just getting worse. Now his dad had started cutting the crossword puzzles out of the newspapers and burning them in the fireplace. That's why William had started locking his bedroom door. So his father wouldn't discover all the stuff he had hidden in his room.

If his father only knew how William felt some days. Sometimes all he could see around him were codes. Anything could actually be a code: a yard, a house, a car, everything he saw on TV or read in a book. They were all puzzles, and his brain took over. It could happen when he looked at a tree or the pattern in some wallpaper. Sometimes it was like things dissolved right before his eyes so that he saw each individual component and where it fit in. He'd been this way for as long as he could remember, and he often got in trouble because of it. That's why he was happiest on his own. Preferably in his room, with the door locked, where he was in full control.

William stood there looking at the big desk, his grandfather's desk. The desktop was made of dark ebony, one of the hardest woods in the world. In each corner there were carvings of demonlike faces, grimacing and sticking out their tongues.

William had been scared of the desk when he was little. But gradually as he got older, he became curious. The whole desktop was covered with strange symbols. William imagined that they were secret messages from his grandfather, who was one of the best cryptologists in the world. But William hadn't managed to decipher the symbols yet. He hoped that someday he would understand them, that he would understand what his grandfather had written, and why.

"WE'RE EATING NOW!" his mother yelled again.

"I'm coming!" William replied. And in two easy steps he was out of the room.

"Aren't you hungry?" his mother asked.

"Not really," William responded, pushing his plate away.

His father swallowed. "You sit around too much," he said. "When I was your age, we never just sat around. We played soccer, ran around outside, stole fruit off the neighbors' trees. Look at you. You're skin and bones."

William tried to ignore him. He knew his dad was right. He *was* skin and bones. But he was stronger than he looked. He always had been. No one in his class could do more push-ups than him. Even his PE teacher had trouble keeping up when he got going.

William glanced at the folded newspaper and pair of scissors sitting on his dad's lap. Recently his father had started cutting even more out of the newspapers than the crosswords. Ever since ads had started showing up about the Impossible Exhibit that was coming to the History of Science Museum. His father was trying as hard as he could to keep William away from it.

But what his father didn't know was that William's class was planning a field trip to the exhibit. His mom had told William he could go if he promised not to say anything to his father. And didn't touch any of the artifacts. It was as if his mom understood how much it meant to him, as if she recognized the tingle William felt every time he thought about the code no one had been able to crack, as if she knew he'd been dreaming about the exhibit ever since he'd first heard of the Impossible Puzzle.

After his dad had left the table, William and his mother sat there for a few more minutes. "Your teacher Mr. Turnbull is very concerned about the museum field trip tomorrow," she said. "And so am I, actually. Living in hiding for so long has been hard for all of us, but we really can't draw attention to ourselves. You know that."

William didn't respond. Mr. Turnbull had hated him ever since William had corrected him in class one day.

"Look at me, William," she said sternly.

He turned and looked at her.

"Promise me you're going to behave yourself tomorrow!" she pleaded. "Can you promise me that? We can't draw attention to ourselves!"

William knew he was going to have a hard time keeping his hands off the Impossible Puzzle. But he also knew that he couldn't do anything that would give them away.

"I promise," he said, and felt a twinge in his stomach.

3

"Hello, and welcome to an exciting day at the History of
Science Museum," said a tall, nervous-looking woman
who greeted them outside the museum. It looked as if
she had been waiting for a while. Her nose was as red as a
tomato, and she was really shivering. She jumped up and
down a little to keep warm while Mr. Turnbull tried to get
the class to settle down. "My name is Edna and I'll be your
guide today." She nervously straightened her skirt. "You're
a little late, and, unfortunately, the Impossible Exhibit is
just closing. But of course you have the whole rest of the
museum."

William stiffened. It couldn't be true. They were too late.

"Since you didn't quite make the Impossible Exhibit,
we'll start with the science word puzzles. Everyone should

take one sheet of paper from the table just inside the doors there," said Edna. "It'll work best if you do it in pairs."

It only took a few seconds for the students to team up with their usual partners. William was still frozen to the spot, paralyzed with disappointment.

"Come on, William, we don't have all day," Mr. Turnbull continued.

William nodded slightly. Then his anger flared. Word puzzles? No way. He was here to see the Impossible Puzzle.

"We'll meet by the exit in one hour," squeaked Edna, opening the large oak doors of the museum.

The class stormed noisily up the front steps. A girl bumped into Edna, knocking her down. Edna sat there on the step, dazed. Mr. Turnbull rushed over to her. She held out her arm so he could help her up.

But Mr. Turnbull hurried right by. "No running . . . WALK!" he yelled at the top of his lungs, and kept going into the museum without so much as looking at her.

William stopped in front of Edna and took her hand. He helped her up. "Thank you," she said, brushing off her skirt.

"You're welcome," said William, smiling meekly. He hesitated a moment.

"Is the Impossible Exhibit totally closed?" he asked.

"They're at maximum capacity down there. We can't let anyone else in, fire marshal's orders," Edna said.

William nodded and proceeded through the doors.

He noticed two men taking down a poster next to the stairs. It said IMPOSSIBLE EXHIBIT—DOWNSTAIRS.

He glanced over at Mr. Turnbull. He was busy with a boy whose hand was stuck in a steam engine. A museum guard had come over to help.

William smiled. Mr. Turnbull had his hands full. Now was his chance to get into the Impossible Exhibit.

William walked down the stairs and stopped. Two enormous guards in gray suits were blocking the doorway. People were packed into the room beyond like sardines. One of the guards was busy with an angry little man who wanted to enter. The little man waved his ticket under the guard's nose.

"I already paid. You can't refuse to let me in if I have a ticket," he yelled.

"Then you should have been here earlier. We can't let any more people in. The exhibit is at maximum capacity." The guard pointed at the crowd behind him to emphasize his point.

"Look at me. I'm only four foot nine. I weigh one hundred ten pounds. No one is going to notice one way or the other whether I'm out here or in there," the man argued.

"Sorry," the other guard said firmly, folding his arms across his chest.

The little man stood there for a few seconds. William saw him clenching his hands into fists like a stubborn four-year-old. His face got redder, and it looked as if he was about to explode.

Then he turned around and started up the stairs. William walked over to the guards.

"Excuse me," he said as innocently as he could. The two men glanced down at him.

"I'm here with my class, and we're supposed to be in there," he said, pointing into the code exhibit.

"Is your class in there?" one of the guards asked.

"Um . . . yeah," William said tentatively.

"Do you have a stamp?"

William stood there. He was about to say something when a shape suddenly came flying through the air and hit one of the guards with a smack.

"LET ME IN! LET ME IN! LET ME IN!" yelled the little man, hanging around the guard's neck and trying to climb over his head to enter the exhibit.

"Get him off of me," the guard yelled. "Get him off of me!"

The other guard rushed over, grabbed the little man's legs, and tried to pull him off his colleague. But the little guy clung to the guard's neck like an angry octopus.

"He's stronger than he looks, Håvard. Tickle him under the arms—maybe he'll let go!" yelled the guard.

"Tickle him yourself, Svein!" the other guard cried back, flailing his arms around.

Several other guards arrived to help. They were all so preoccupied that none of them noticed William slip through the open doors.

Soon William was standing in the middle of a large room, surrounded by people. His body tingled. He had to find a spot where he could get a good view. It was only a question of time before Mr. Turnbull discovered that he was missing, and once he had, he would move heaven and earth to find him. The Impossible Exhibit would be the first place he'd check.

"Only five minutes left to decipher the world's most difficult puzzle!" a voice announced over the PA system. "Many have tried, but none have succeeded. Yet."

William glanced around. On the wall at the far end of the room he spotted a screen on which big, red numbers were counting down. A poster with a picture of the Impossible Puzzle was hanging over the countdown clock. William pushed his way forward. He didn't have any plans to solve the Impossible Puzzle. He just wanted to see it. Preferably when someone else was trying to solve it. His pulse sped up, his adrenaline pumped.

A couple of minutes later William had managed to push

his way through the crowd and was now standing in front of a small stage.

There was a chair and a table on the stage. A thin man in his midforties was sitting in the chair. His long, blond hair was pulled back into a ponytail. He was leaning over the table, twisting sections of a metal cylinder. Little beads of sweat kept appearing on his forehead. He was breathing hard, constantly casting nervous glances up at the digital countdown clock on the wall above him.

A chubby man in a tight suit was fidgeting nervously next to the table. William recognized him from TV. His name was Ludo Kläbbert, and he was a kind of jack-of-all-trades comedian. Ludo raised the microphone to his mouth and glanced up at the clock as he started to count down.

"Ten . . . nine . . . eight . . . seven . . ."

Soon everyone in the room was counting with him. It looked as if the long-haired man was going to pass out.

"Five . . . four . . . three . . . two . . . one . . . zero!" cried Ludo. "Time's up! Have you solved it, Vektor Hansen?" Ludo walked over to the sweaty man at the table.

Vektor Hansen carefully set the cylinder down and shook his head in shame.

"Even Vektor Hansen, the man with the highest IQ in all of Norway, can't solve the Impossible Puzzle. This truly is a tough nut to crack!" cried Ludo.

Suddenly Hansen stood up and snatched the microphone.

"This is some kind of scam! A bad joke! There is no solution. It can't be solved," Vektor barked grumpily into the microphone.

He picked up the Impossible Puzzle and raised it threateningly over his head, as if he was about to smash it to the floor.

"This is nonsense!" he yelled.

Ludo waved over two uniformed guards who hopped onto the stage, snatched the cylinder out of Vektor's hands, and handed it to Ludo before pulling Vektor down off the stage with them. A few people laughed, and others booed.

"I'm still a lot smarter than all of you put together!" yelled Hansen as he was carried out the door next to the stage. "You're all just a bunch of hicks compared to me. I'm brilliant!" The door banged shut, and it was quiet in the room.

Ludo stood onstage with the Impossible Puzzle in his hands. A murmur ran through the crowd.

"Is it just a trick?" a voice called out.

"Typical!" yelled someone else.

"No, no!" said Ludo, waving his hands in the air.

"Prove it then!" another voice called from the crowd. "Let one more person try!"

Ludo glanced nervously around. His eyes came to rest on a serious woman with stern-looking eyeglasses, who was standing next to the stage. She nodded.

"Okay, but just one more. The time is actually up. Who wants to try?" cried Ludo, nervously brushing the sweat off his face with the back of his hand.

The room became completely silent. A couple of people murmured, while others shook their heads.

"No one?" asked Ludo.

"William!" a loud voice suddenly called out.

William turned and saw Mr. Turnbull pushing his way through the crowd, pointing at William, who was standing next to the stage.

And then everyone turned to look at William. "Yes, let him try it," someone cried out. Ludo looked at William in surprise.

"A kid? Why not? You never know." He gestured to William.

"No, wait!" yelled Mr. Turnbull. "I didn't mean . . ."

But it was already too late. Ludo had pulled William up onto the stage and placed the Impossible Puzzle into his hands. William peered at the shiny cylinder. He couldn't believe his eyes.

"No, not . . . ," yelled Mr. Turnbull. He tried to make his way up onto the stage, but the guards pulled him back down.

Ludo glanced at William.

"Would you like to try? Some of the sharpest minds in the world have tried without succeeding."

William shook his head. "No, I don't think—"

"Oh, come on; it can't hurt to try," Ludo teased with a smile.

Ludo turned to the audience and limply waved his index finger around. "What do you say, folks? Would you like him to give it a try?"

The crowd broke into spontaneous applause. William looked at the Impossible Puzzle.

He had never seen a single one of the symbols on the cylinder before. They weren't letters or numbers. But then something began to happen. The way it always did. It began in his stomach, like a warm ache. Then it spread up into his chest and out into his hands and his head. It was as if things started happening on their own. William tried to set the device down, to let go of it, but it was too late.

It was as if the small parts in the cylinder came to life in his hands. Some of the pieces seemed to shrink, others changed color. Some started glowing while others grew so dark that they almost disappeared. The symbols came loose from the cylinder and floated around his head like a swarm of butterflies. He followed them with his eyes. Then his hands began working. They twisted and turned the little components. His fingers moved faster and faster. "Click . . . click . . . click . . . ," the device said.

Then time and place ceased to exist.

It wasn't until a tremendous outburst of cheering

practically raised the roof of the great exhibition hall that William snapped out of his trance and looked down at the device he was still holding in his hands. But it wasn't a cylinder anymore. It was split in two. And on one part there was a brass plate engraved with the word CONGRATULATIONS!

William couldn't get a single word out. He just stood there staring at the brass plate inside the cylinder. His eyes saw what it said, but his brain refused to believe it. *It must be broken,* he thought. *I didn't solve it . . . I broke it.* He looked at Ludo, who stood next to him, speechless. After that he glanced at Mr. Turnbull, who put his hands up to his head and collapsed onto the floor in front of the stage.

William tried to put the pieces back together again, but it didn't work. He tried again. And again.

It must be broken. It must!

The museum director's office was cramped. William was sitting in a chair in front of the director, who was studying the Impossible Puzzle. William glanced at the window. Journalists and other curious onlookers had gathered in the street outside. He could hear them yelling. William glanced back at the museum director, who kept turning the device over. He pulled out a magnifying glass, which he put to his eye, and brought the two pieces right up to his face.

"Hm . . . hm," he mumbled. "It doesn't look like it was pried open in any way." He regarded William over the top of his eyeglasses.

William looked down at the floor, as if he'd done

something wrong. And he had, of course. He'd promised his mother he wouldn't touch the puzzle.

"You realize we're going to have to notify the media? People all over the world will want to know what you did," the museum director said.

All the color drained from William's face.

"Is that really necessary?" he asked with a gulp.

This was a complete disaster. His mom was going to have a breakdown. And his dad . . . William couldn't even begin to imagine how his father was going to react.

The museum director stared thoughtfully at William for a while.

"You're under eighteen, so, strictly speaking, we need your parents' permission before we talk to the press. Could you give me your mom or dad's phone number?"

William squirmed in the chair and shook his head. "It would be best if I told them," he said. "My parents don't really like attention that much."

The museum director mulled that over for a moment and then shrugged. "All right then," he said with a smile. "I'll have someone from the museum drive you home. You can sneak out the back way."

William stood up and moved toward the door.

"William," the museum director said. William stopped and turned around. "You know how incredible this is, right?"

★ ★ ★

A white delivery truck stopped at the driveway. The door opened and William hopped out. He walked toward the house, took a deep breath as if he were about to dive underwater, put his hand on the doorknob, and entered. He heard quiet voices from the living room.

His mother was sitting on the sofa, and his father was next to her in his wheelchair. The radio was on in the background. They looked up when William walked in. The silence seemed to go on forever.

"William," his father finally said.

William didn't know what to say. His father beckoned him over and turned up the volume on the radio.

"And now back to the History of Science Museum and the sensational news about the Impossible Puzzle. This code, which up until today had been considered the hardest in the world, has now been deciphered. We still don't know the identity of the person who did it," the reporter said, "but we talked to someone who was present when it happened. And now over to you, Aslak."

His mother's hands were trembling. She clasped them together in her lap to try to calm them, but it didn't seem to help. William gulped and looked at the floor. He knew he was in trouble.

"I'm standing here outside the History of Science Museum with Tordis Voffel, who was present when this amazing feat took place," the reporter announced. "Tordis, can you tell us what happened?"

A woman cleared her throat a couple of times before she started speaking.

"I was there with my grandson. He likes codes and things like that. We were about to leave after that high-IQ guy had to give up. We wanted to beat the rush to the café. I'd promised Halvor I'd buy him an ice cream. Chocolate, he's not that fond of—"

"And what happened?" the interviewer interrupted impatiently.

"Well, then suddenly there was a boy standing onstage," the woman said with a sort of mock dismay in her voice. "I don't know where he came from. He just appeared as if out of nowhere. I thought it was a little strange that they would let a child try, especially after the other geniuses had to give up."

"What happened?" the interviewer asked.

"Before we knew it, he'd cracked the code. And then there was complete chaos in the room. I grabbed Halvor and pulled him out of there. I mean, you hear about people being trampled to death, and besides I had promised him I would—"

William's father turned off the radio and sat there for a moment without saying anything.

"Was it you?" he finally asked.

"I . . . ," William began, but couldn't get anything else out. His voice was shaking too much.

His mother began to cry.

"It doesn't matter now. We have to pack!" his father said, driving his wheelchair out of the room.

6

William went up to the top floor. He proceeded down the hallway and stopped when he came to the end. He ran a hand over the pinewood paneling on the wall. His index finger stopped at a large knothole in the paneling. He wiggled his finger into the hole and pressed something. There was a click from inside the wall. Then the ceiling creaked, and a trapdoor opened up.

He'd made the secret entrance himself. William climbed up the ladder and disappeared through the opening into the attic.

There was just enough room beneath the sloped roof for him to stand upright. Apart from one low bookshelf, the attic was almost empty, with just a few old cardboard boxes in one corner. William turned on a wall lamp and walked over to the bookshelf. There weren't many books, but these were the ones that meant the most to him. William had no idea how many times he'd read them, hundreds maybe. He knew them by heart. And what made them extra special was that they were full of his grandfather's notes. When he read them, he felt like his grandfather was talking to him. He had learned so much from these books. Things you never heard about in school. He slid his fingers along the spines: *Secrets of the Cave Paintings, The Pyramids: The Biggest Codes in the World, Atlantis: They Knew More Than We Do, The Earth Isn't What You Think.*

William sat down on the area rug and pulled out a leather-bound photo album, which was hidden beneath the shelf. He gently ran his finger over the first page. Grandfather's handwriting was just barely visible: *Excavation Documentation, Part 89.*

William slowly browsed through the album. He glanced at the pictures his grandfather had taken at various archeological digs. He had been everywhere. But William had no idea what he'd been looking for or what he'd found. Those were the kinds of questions he so wished he could ask his grandfather. He peered at the old photographs his grandfather had taken. There were pictures from all over the world: everything from famous places like the pyramids in Egypt to secret sites in the Amazon and Tibet. Next to the photographs Grandfather had noted the place and the time, but never what they'd been looking for.

The ladder creaked. William looked up and saw his mother. He closed the photo album.

"May I join you?" she asked.

William nodded.

His mom sat down next to him. She sat there for a while with her hands in her lap.

William tried to find the words to express what he wanted to say but couldn't.

"There's so much you don't know. We wanted to protect you, didn't want you to walk around feeling scared," his mother began.

"What do you mean?" William asked.

"Your father and I . . . we've always known it couldn't last forever. You're too much like your grandfather," she said, stroking William's hair. "I think it's time you knew what happened in London eight years ago," his mother said, and swallowed dryly. "The reason we're not safe."

"Are we in danger now?" he asked meekly.

"Yes, I think we are," she said.

They sat there in silence for a bit. William ran his hands over the album.

"Can I see?" his mom asked.

William nodded. His mom smiled at the sight of Grandfather's ornate handwriting.

"Time goes so quickly. It feels like I just saw him yesterday."

She turned the page. The next picture showed an over-grown Incan pyramid surrounded by thick jungle.

"Your grandfather loved his work. He was always on the go. I can barely remember him being home when I was a kid. Maybe that's why he took such good care of you before he vanished. You meant the world to him, William."

"What happened to him?"

"We don't know for sure. He disappeared right after we moved to Norway."

"But why did we move?" William asked. His mother looked at him.

"It had to do with your grandfather's work. We don't know why, but he thought our lives were in danger and sent us here. We had to start a whole new life. No one could even know we were related to your grandfather. That's why we don't have any pictures of him on the walls, and why we don't talk about him very much."

"But who's after us? How can it be dangerous for people to find out that I solved a puzzle?"

"That wasn't just any old puzzle, William. It was the hardest one in the world. You and your grandfather are probably the only people in the world who could have done it. It's only a question of time before they find us now." She turned to the next page in the album. The picture was of an old brass casing full of gears and levers. Under the picture, in Grandfather's handwriting, it said *Computer, Greece. (Age: indefinite).*

"And there's one more thing. . . ." His mom hesitated.

"What?" William asked.

"Well, you know how your father doesn't like to talk about how he got paralyzed. . . ."

William nodded.

"You know he was in a car accident?" his mother continued.

"Yes," said William.

"Well, he wasn't the only one in the car."

"He wasn't?" William exclaimed.

"No," she said. "You were in the car with him, William."

"Me?" William's head started to swim.

"You only barely survived. I thought you were going to die. That's what the doctors said, that you weren't going to make it." His mother wiped a tear from the corner of her eye.

"But then how did I survive?" asked William, his voice quavering.

His mom glanced down at the photo album. She was quiet for what seemed like forever.

"Your grandfather was out of the country, working. When he heard about the accident, he caught the first flight home. He sat by your bedside every night for weeks . . . and then you suddenly started to improve. The doctors didn't know what was going on. Your grandfather said it was a miracle."

William tried to put his thoughts in order. Had he almost

died? And his grandfather had watched over him . . . and then he recovered?

He glanced back up at his mother and saw how her body was trembling.

"Mom, who are we hiding from?" he asked. "Does it have anything to do with the accident?"

"I don't know, William," she said, and stood up.

"But . . . ?" William began, then stopped. It was clear that his mother didn't want to talk about it anymore.

"We're leaving tomorrow. It isn't safe for us here anymore."

"Where are we going?" William asked.

"Far away from here," she said, and then vanished down the hatch in the floor.

William was lying on top of his comforter with his clothes on. He was staring at the ceiling. It was three thirty in the morning, and he was still wide awake. He knew he wasn't going to be able to fall asleep. There were too many thoughts rampaging around in his head. He was thinking about what his mother had said about the accident and how he'd almost died. How had he survived? Did his grandfather's disappearance have anything to do with that? Every time he thought about what had happened at the museum, his stomach ached. Now the whole world would know who solved the Impossible Puzzle. It was his fault they had to go on the run again.

William heard his parents downstairs in the living room. They were packing up the essentials. They were going to leave as soon as it was light out.

William sat up in bed and looked around at his dark bedroom. Was it colder in here? He got up and walked over to the window but stopped when he stepped on something hard. He glanced down and spotted it on the floor in front of him. He squatted. It was a beetle, lying on its back with its little legs up in the air. William carefully poked it with his finger. It didn't react. He picked it up and put it in his hand.

William walked over to the desk and set the beetle on the desktop. He opened one of the drawers and pulled out a big magnifying glass. He sat there, staring at the little creature. This was no ordinary beetle. It was made of tiny metal pieces that were held together by even tinier screws. It was a mechanical beetle! And one of the most beautiful and most advanced things he'd ever seen.

How had it gotten in? He glanced over at that window and noticed a small hole in the glass pane. The beetle suddenly twitched, startling William. He leaped off the chair and stumbled backward until he hit the wall.

The little beetle popped up, flipped over, and landed on its legs. Then it jumped off the edge of the desk and landed on the floor with a clank. It stood there watching William for a little while before it again picked up speed and scurried around the room. It stopped when it encountered a pencil under the desk. The beetle grasped the pencil, proceeded over to William, and set the pencil on the floor in front of him. It was acting like a playful dog. William smiled and picked up the pencil.

"Do you want to play?"

The beetle jumped up and down on the floor. William tossed the pencil. It hit the wall and landed on the floor. The beetle ran over, picked the pencil up again, and delivered it back at William's feet. William grinned, impressed.

"Wow, you're fast," he said. Then he picked up the pencil and threw it a little harder.

The pencil hit the doorframe and landed in the hallway. The beetle darted out, but this time it didn't come back. It stayed in the hallway, peering in at William. "Come," said William.

But the beetle didn't come. It restlessly tapped a leg on the wood floor, as if it wanted William to come out into the hallway.

"Come here!" William said, but when the beetle didn't move, he approached it cautiously. "Stay, staaaay," he said in a calm voice.

He stopped right in front of the beetle and squatted down slowly. He held out his hand, but right before he could grab it, the beetle darted down the hall toward the stairs.

"No, no, no," whispered William, rushing after it.

The beetle paused at the top of the stairs and set down the pencil. William stopped a few yards away from it.

"Don't go downstairs," William pleaded.

But the beetle didn't listen and kept going down the stairs. William leaned forward and peered into the dark hallway on the floor below. Where did the beetle go?

He heard his parents talking quietly. William crept farther down the stairs and cautiously leaned over the railing.

"I don't know," he heard his dad say. "It could be a coincidence, of course, but I don't think we can take any chances."

"Did you talk to the Institute?" his mom asked.

"Yes, they're on their way," his dad said. "Obviously they already knew about what had happened at the museum. I'm quite certain they're the ones behind the whole Impossible Puzzle world tour."

"Trying to track him down?" his mom asked.

"It's in his genes. They knew it was only a question of time before he took the bait," his dad said.

"Sending him back to England, though . . . Isn't there any other option?" his mom asked.

"It's better to get him out of the country for a while. We can't take any chances. The Institute is probably the safest place for him right now," his dad said.

"I'm so tired of this, tired of hiding. I want my old life back." His mom sounded like she was crying.

"Me too, but we can't take any chances," his father repeated.

A sound drew William's attention away from the conversation. He peered into the dark hallway. He had lived in this house for most of his life. And he knew it well. Especially the sounds it made. The way the walls creaked in a storm. And how the roof crackled on a hot summer day. But the sound he heard now was a new one. It was a dry clicking sound. Like metal on metal. And it came from the hallway below.

Click . . . click . . . click . . .

William leaned even farther over the railing and squinted into the darkness down there.

Click . . . click . . . click . . .

Suddenly he spotted a large shadow, which moved along the wall and then disappeared. William was about to yell, but he was interrupted by his father, who screamed at the top of his lungs from the living room, "WILLIAM! GET OUT OF THE HOUSE! RUN! RUN!"

William stood there on the stairs, completely paralyzed. He heard his mother wail, and then his father shouted again, "RUN, WILLIAM, RUN!"

William turned and ran down the hall. He dashed into his room and shut the door behind him. The whole house was shaking.

Then he heard heavy footsteps on the stairs. The stairs creaked and thumped as the footsteps approached. They stopped just outside his door.

William stood totally still, holding his breath, listening. Nothing.

Not a sound.

It was completely quiet. Way too quiet.

Then he heard a tapping sound from somewhere in front of him. He looked up, scanning the room with scared eyes. The window!

He darted to it just before the door was smashed to smithereens behind him. He yanked up the window and flung himself out into the darkness.

William landed heavily in the snow.

He tumbled forward and ended up doing a somer-
sault before he could get back onto his feet and run away
through the yard in just his socks. Getting away was the
only thought on his mind.

Rumbling and cracking noises came from the house behind
him. It sounded like someone was destroying his bedroom.

A couple of seconds later William was sprinting across
the snow-covered road. He heard the window shatter, and
something heavy landed in the yard. Then the wooden
fence exploded into kindling behind him.

Something was after him, something big.

Click . . . click . . . click . . . the same sound he had heard
in the hallway.

William jumped into a random yard. He wondered whether he ought to knock on one of the neighbors' doors but quickly rejected that idea. He stumbled on, continuing onto a street he didn't recognize. His feet were hurting now. His lungs were aching, and the muscles in his thighs burned. It was only a question of time before his legs gave out. He didn't know where he was headed, only that he had to keep going. Suddenly the ground fell away beneath him, and he tumbled down a slope. He struggled to his feet and looked around, gasping for breath. He was at the edge of a big field. He glanced back. There was no sign of whatever was after him. Had he escaped?

William struggled to get his thoughts in order. His body was trembling from the cold, and it had started to snow again. Big snowflakes wafted down from the dark sky.

William kept moving across the field, but the deep snow made it difficult. He stopped at a tall chain-link fence at the far end of the field and looked at what lay beyond. It seemed to be some kind of abandoned industrial property. He climbed over the fence and headed for one of the dilapidated buildings.

The door was missing. William went in. Rusty water dripped from the roof. A truck with no wheels sat in one corner. Legs trembling, William headed for the truck and peeked inside. He tried the door. It was locked. He looked around and spotted a big adjustable wrench on the warehouse floor. He used that to break the truck's window and then climbed in.

His body ached, and his head felt as if it was exploding. He just had to make it through the night. He could find help first thing in the morning. His first order of business would be to find his parents. Had they made it out? And . . . William noticed something move past the door of the warehouse. He sat up and leaned toward the windshield, peering into the darkness for several minutes. Nothing. Just snowflakes drifting down. William leaned back in the seat again.

Suddenly it was as if a bomb had gone off right above him. A large iron beam crashed onto the hood of the truck with such force that it shattered the windshield. Metal and sheets of corrugated iron were raining down around the truck.

Then everything grew quiet again.

William cautiously leaned forward and glanced up. The whole roof of the building had been torn off. It was snowing too hard for him to be able to see if there was anything up there.

Something moved over by the door. Two silhouettes entered the building. One of them was carrying something that looked like a gun, which pulsed with a blue light. The man raised the gun and pointed it at William, cringing in the cab of the truck.

Suddenly a large iron claw thundered onto the hood,

grabbed hold of the truck, and yanked it up into the air with tremendous force. William screamed and clung to the steering wheel. The last thing he saw was a ray of blue light hitting the truck.

Then everything went black.

William was lying on something soft. His body rocked gently
back and forth. A faint hum lured him out of sleep. What
had just happened? Something about snow . . . a bang and
blue light . . . Then suddenly he remembered his father's
frightened voice yelling, "RUN, WILLIAM, RUN!" And
the little beetle scurrying away, and the truck . . . William sat
up and looked around.

He was in the backseat of a car that was driving really
fast on a deserted highway. William put his hands to his
head and felt a bandage on his forehead. He checked the
rest of his body. Apart from being a little stiff and sore, it
seemed like he was more or less intact.

He leaned forward and peeked through the window sep-
arating him from the front of the car. There were two men

with red hair sitting there. Could they be the two silhouettes he'd seen in the warehouse? He felt the panic rising. Who were they? What did they want with him? Were these the men they'd been hiding from for the last eight years?

He made eye contact with one of them in the rearview mirror. The man regarded him with small, cold eyes before looking away again. William leaned back in the seat. If they wanted to kill him, he'd already be dead by now, right? Maybe they'd saved him from whatever was after him? Cautiously he knocked on the glass divider in front of him. The men didn't react. He knocked a couple more times, each time a little harder.

"WHO ARE YOU?" he yelled. But they didn't turn around.

Suddenly the glass in front of him went dark, and then the image of a beautiful woman with dark hair and big, blue eyes gave him a friendly smile.

"Welcome, William Wenton," she said in a silky voice.

William stared at her. William *Wenton*?

How did she know his real name? William leaned forward and studied the crystal-clear picture. The lady smiled at him with dazzling white teeth.

"My name is Malin, and it's my pleasure to welcome you to the Institute for Post-Human Research," she said. "In a little while we will be arriving at Gardermoen Airport outside Oslo. From there our private plane will bring you to Heathrow Airport. Then your journey will continue to the Institute, which is idyllically situated in rural England. You will receive more information on the plane. Until then, I wish you a pleasant trip," she said with a smile.

"Thanks," mumbled William.

"In the meantime, I have a greeting from your parents," Malin continued. "They're in safe hands."

In safe hands, William repeated to himself. That meant that his parents were alive. Tears sprang to his eyes. Before he could say anything, his mom and dad appeared on the screen. They were sitting in the backseat of a car that looked like the one William was in.

"William . . . ," his mother began, struggling against tears. "William, honey. This wasn't how it was supposed to be. I'm just so happy you weren't hurt or . . ." His mother paused. She swallowed and wiped away her tears. "It won't be too long before we're together again."

His mother glanced at his father and took his hand.

"There's so much we should have told you, William. But we thought it was best that you knew as little as possible. They'll explain everything to you when you arrive at the Institute," his father said with a smile.

"I love you so much, sweetie," his mom said.

"I love you, too," whispered William before the picture flickered a couple of times and disappeared.

William stared at the glass in front of him, as if he

expected the image of his parents to come back. But it didn't. He thought about what they'd said. What was this "Institute"? Should he ask the two men? Surely they were from the Institute, but they didn't really seem like the chatty type. That would have to wait. All William could do was trust that his parents knew what they were talking about, that he was in safe hands, and that they were all right too. He leaned back against the soft seat, a little more relaxed now. He watched the dark countryside passing by.

A short time later they pulled into an off-limits area at Gardermoen Airport, where a big, shiny passenger plane sat waiting for them. A man in a pilot's uniform waved to them before disappearing into the cockpit. The car stopped right in front of the nose of the plane. Then William heard the sound of electric motors as the front of the plane opened, like the jaw of a gigantic shark, and when the jaw was wide open, the car drove on board.

10

William had the entire airplane cabin to himself, and it wasn't just any old airplane cabin. Everything around him was shiny and white. There were no seats, just two big, white sofas. He was sitting on one of them, buckled in securely. It was like sitting in some kind of luxury spaceship, William thought.

The plane was already in the air, and down below he could see a layer of clouds. It was quiet in the cabin; the only sound was the distant whir of the engines outside.

William jumped when the table in front of him suddenly pulled apart and a screen rose up from between the two halves. A blue logo that said *Institute for Post-Human Research* appeared. The logo rotated a couple of time before vanishing, replaced by Malin. She smiled at him with her dazzling white teeth.

"Welcome aboard, William Wenton. We at the Institute for Post-Human Research warmly welcome you as a new candidate," she said in a pleasant although monotone voice. "We hope you've had a pleasant journey thus far. You will be offered food and beverage service soon."

"Candidate?" William said.

"One of our information bots will answer any questions you might have soon," she continued as if he hadn't spoken. "In the meantime, please enjoy a virtual tour of the Institute."

Pictures of an enormous white building rolled across the screen in front of him. "The Institute was founded in 1967 and has worked tirelessly since then on research that will benefit all of humanity," Malin continued.

The building was every bit as white and glossy as the airplane William was sitting in. But the foundation was made of stone and looked really old.

"Here at the Institute for Post-Human Research the past and the present merge together in a perfect union. The Institute specializes in researching biotechnology and artificial intelligence," Malin continued. "Every year the Institute admits a group of candidates who have distinguished themselves in the field of code breaking, cryptography, and problem solving. As a candidate at the Institute for Post-Human Research, you will enjoy the use of all our facilities. We will be at your service to help make your time here as productive as possible. Thank you for your attention."

Then the screen went blank and sank back down into the table.

William sat there wondering what he'd just seen. The Institute for Post-Human Research? Why in the world was he being sent there?

And what was a candidate?

William heard a door sliding open at the front of the cabin. He leaned forward and spotted a wheeled serving cart heading toward him. The cart stopped with a sudden squeak.

"We can offer you whole wheat or white bread with synthetic ham or synthetic tofu," announced the cart as a robot arm shot out from the side and pointed at a selection of bottles and baguettes on a tray. "If you're thirsty, you can select between synthetic water, synthetic orange juice, or Mars juice."

"Why is everything synthetic?" William asked, leaning forward to get a better look.

"Because that's the way it is," said the cart impatiently.

William hesitated as his eyes scanned the bottles and the plastic-wrapped baguettes. They didn't look synthetic at all.

"So what'll it be," said the cart, and wheeled a little closer.

"Uh, a whole wheat with ham and Mars juice," William said, bewildered.

"An excellent choice. The Mars juice is at its best this time of day," the cart said as a lid popped up and a robot arm placed the sandwich and a glass of purple juice on the table in front of him.

"Enjoy your meal," the cart said. "A trash bot will come clean up once you're finished."

The cart squeaked as it lurched back to the front of the plane in reverse at high speed.

"But . . . ?" William said, confused.

"A trash bot will come to clean up. Take as much time as you need. No hurry," called the cart, and then disappeared through the doorway.

William shook his head in irritation and peered at the food in front of him. He unwrapped the sandwich and smelled it. What in the world was synthetic ham? And Mars juice?

He took a tentative bite and chewed. The ham tasted exactly like normal ham, only better. He took another bite and another. Soon he was wolfing it down. This had to be the best sandwich he'd ever eaten.

Afterward he took a sip of the Mars juice, which had changed color now and was red. It tasted like sweet strawberry-and-vanilla ice cream. *Weird,* William thought, and took another swig. Now it tasted like oranges, and he realized the juice wasn't red anymore. It was orange.

Then the door opened again, and the same cart came wheeling toward him. "Trash?" it asked politely.

"Aren't you the same cart that—"

"No, I am not!" the offended cart protested as a mechanical hand shot up from a lid and snatched the empty plastic container and napkin. "Thank you. Enjoy the rest of your trip," the trash bot said, backing away.

"But I was just wondering . . ."

"An information bot will answer any questions you have soon," the cart said, disappearing through the door.

William leaned back, closed his eyes, and tried to collect his thoughts. Yet again he heard the sound of the door at the front of the cabin opening. William looked up. That same cart was coming back down the center aisle. It stopped with a jerk next to him.

"Questions?" it quickly asked.

"Yes, are you the serving cart, the trash cart, *and* the information cart all in one?" William asked.

"If you have existential questions, you must bring these up with the philosoph-bot! I can send him out next. Was there anything else?"

"Why am I here?" William asked.

The cart said, "Uh . . ." but then remained silent. The little blinking lights went out. It almost seemed as if it had turned itself off. Or short-circuited.

"Hello?" William said cautiously, knocking on the cart.

All he got in response was a hollow, metallic sound. It was like knocking on the side of an empty toaster.

The cart just sat there.

William looked around, confused.

Then suddenly its lights came back on, and the cart hummed to life again. "Apologies for the delay," the cart said. "Your questions will be answered when you arrive at headquarters."

William slumped back in the seat. He was too tired to argue with a cart.

"Was there anything else? I do have a great deal of information about air travel, waste management, and synthetic-food production."

"No thanks. I'm good," William said.

"Enjoy the rest of your trip. We'll be landing in one hour and thirteen minutes," the cart said, reversing away. "If I were you, I would get some shut-eye," it called before disappearing through the door at the end of the aisle.

William turned his head and looked out the window. Outside was only darkness. And sleep was the furthest thing from his mind right now. He was tired, but his head was drowning in questions.

Where was he headed? And what had happened to his parents?

11

William awoke with a start and looked around in fear.

He was lying in the backseat of a car again. The last thing he remembered was getting back into the car and driving off the plane. Then they had traveled through endless roads deep into the English countryside. He must have finally given in to tiredness and dozed off.

The car came to a stop in front of a large stone staircase. William blinked the sleepiness out of his eyes and sat up.

He recognized the building from the video he'd seen on the plane. It looked even bigger in real life. Suddenly there was a knock on the car window, and a gloved hand gestured for him to get out. The door slid open, and William took a cautious step down. He discovered that someone had put a pair of new shoes on his feet.

"Welcome, William Wenton," said a tall, dark figure, bowing deeply. William just stood there looking at the man, who peered somberly back at him, his face expressionless. He was wearing a black tuxedo with tails, a white shirt, and a blue bow tie. He looked very formal.

"I'm Tim Cutler," he said in a flat voice, straightening up again.

"William," said William, holding out his hand.

"I know," Cutler said. They shook hands. "I'm the chief butler here at the Institute. Where is it all?"

"Where's what?" William asked.

"Your luggage!"

"Oh. I didn't bring anything with me," William said, a little embarrassed, and smiled apologetically.

Cutler looked at him aghast.

"You don't have anything with you?" he cried. "No clean underwear, socks, or anything?"

William shook his head.

"A toothbrush?" Cutler asked.

"I left in a bit of a hurry," William said, feeling his cheeks redden.

"All right," the butler said. "This way, please."

William stood there watching while Cutler removed one glove and then waved his hand back and forth in front of a little red sensor in the door. Cutler lowered his hand

and was putting his glove back on when the door emitted two short clicks and swung open.

"After you," he said, gesturing to William.

William walked in but stopped when someone suddenly yelled, "Watch out!" He looked around but couldn't see where the voice was coming from. Something hit him hard in the legs, and he lost his balance and fell down. William sat up, bewildered, and grabbed his shin.

"You have to watch out!" Cutler said from behind him.

"I'm sorry," William said, looking up.

But now William realized that Cutler wasn't scolding him. He was wagging his index finger at a little electric vacuum cleaner on the floor in front of him.

"Um, sorry. I was on my way to the TV room. *The Terminator* is on," the vacuum cleaner said apologetically as it restlessly scooted back and forth.

"Vacuum cleaners don't watch TV," Cutler said. "Back to the docking station with you. You're going to need all the electricity you can get for tomorrow."

"All right then." The vacuum cleaner turned around and slowly rolled back the way it had come from. "Sorry, man," it mumbled to William as it went by.

"Darn machines," Cutler sniffed, walking on.

William got up and looked around. They were in a large hall. An enormous chandelier hung from the ceiling. A grand staircase stretched up in front of him, leading to the second floor. *That staircase must be as wide as a four-lane highway,* William thought.

"Are you coming?" Cutler called.

William started walking but stopped again when he spotted a square metal box with thin little legs that was coming down the stairs. When the metal box reached the bottom step, it turned around and started going back up.

"What is that?" William asked.

"A step bot," Cutler answered, uninterested.

"What does it do?" William asked.

"It climbs stairs," Cutler said. "Come on. We don't have all day."

"But what's the point of a robot that can only climb stairs?" William asked, trying to keep up with Cutler as he made his way down a long hallway.

"This is a research institution. Most things here are experimental. And often completely impractical."

Cutler stopped beside a tall, flat robot standing motionless by the wall, as if it was trying not to be seen.

"Take this one, for example," Cutler continued. "This is the most useless of them all. An argu-bot," he said, his voice filled with disdain.

"Pure lies and malicious rumors," the argu-bot retorted tersely.

"What does an argu-bot do?" William asked.

"It argues, of course," Cutler said, already starting to move away down the hall.

"Well, it beats being a cheap penguin impersonator in a butler's uniform," the argu-bot snapped back.

Cutler stopped and turned around. "What did you just say?"

"Nothing," the argu-bot said. "Just that you're quite fat considering you're so short!"

Cutler walked right up to the argu-bot and growled between his clenched teeth. "One of these days when you least expect it, I'm going to come pull your plug," he said, sneering wickedly.

"I run on batteries," the robot said.

"Rubbish," Cutler said, pointing to a cord that was plugged into a nearby outlet. "What's that, then?"

"That's for the lamp," the argu-bot said, nodding at a floor lamp next to him.

"Don't you dare!" the lamp said indignantly.

Cutler shook his head and rolled his eyes.

"You see what I mean by useless?" he muttered to William, proceeding down the hallway. "Come on!"

William hurried after Cutler and caught up to him again as they passed a chair where a small, round robot sat dangling its long, thin legs over the edge of the seat.

"I suppose this is a sit bot, then?" William said jokingly.

"You're a quick learner," Cutler said. "I just call him

Humpty Dumpty. Ah, here we are." He stopped in front of a big white door. "You can wait in the library until Mr. Goffman arrives."

Cutler waved his hand in front of the door a couple of times. It slid open with an electric swoosh.

"In you go," Cutler said. "Oh, and watch out for the librarian. He can be a little . . . um . . . unpredictable sometimes."

William looked around. The walls and ceiling were made of shiny stainless steel, the floor, too. The sofa in the corner looked like it had never been sat on. And everything on the desk in front of him was arranged at right angles. He didn't see a single book anywhere. Actually, this didn't look like a library at all.

"Mr. Goffman is just around the corner," a hoarse voice announced.

William turned around but didn't see anyone. He stood there, waiting. He remembered the butler's warning about the librarian.

"I said, Mr. Goffman is just around the corner!" the voice repeated.

"I heard you . . . but, um, where are you?"

"Here, obviously," the voice said, a little irritated.

William heard the hum of an electric motor, but he still couldn't see anyone. "Behind you," the voice said.

William turned around, and now he saw a robot on wheels with four long arms. The robot was just as shiny and glossy as the library. It fit in so well with its surroundings that it was almost completely camouflaged.

"Are you the librarian?"

"Correct," the robot said. "Albert."

"But where are all the . . . ," William began. He looked around, but before he could finish his sentence, one of Albert's long metal arms shot out and pricked William's index finger with a little needle.

"Ow!" William cried. He held up his finger and saw a little drop of red blood.

"Sorry," Albert said as one of his other arms quickly collected the drop of blood with a pipette.

"What are you doing?" William yelled, peering at the robot in dismay.

"Just a little blood test, completely harmless," Albert said, rolling to the side. "There. In the meantime, have a seat on the sofa. Here's something to read while you're waiting. This is a library after all."

Albert held out an e-reader. William hesitated a moment before taking it and sitting on the sofa. He tried to relax when he suddenly felt something yank his hair.

"Ow!" he yelled again, looking at the robot in confusion. Albert was holding a tuft of his hair in one of his hands.

"I'm sorry," Albert said, hiding the tuft of hair behind its back. "Just a completely standard hair sample. But I'm finished now, I promise. No more tests and that's the truth."

William leaned back on the sofa and turned on the e-reader. An overview of the books appeared on the screen. *Alternative Mathematics*, the first one was called. Then there was *Pyramid Theory and Mechanical Origami*. William had to smile. The Institute seemed like a place where he could feel at home.

"Perhaps you've read some of them before," said a deep voice behind him.

William turned and saw an unusually tall, thin man. He was wearing a black suit and leaning on a white cane. His hair was coal black. He regarded William with deep, dark eyes.

"Did you have a pleasant trip?" he asked.

"Yes," William stammered.

"Good," the man said, looking over at Albert. "Albert, did you get what you needed?"

"Yes," said the robot, holding out the pipette and the tuft of William's hair.

"You can leave us," the man said.

Albert wheeled out into the hallway, and the door slid shut behind him. The tall man waited until the door was closed before walking back over to William and holding out his hand.

"Fritz Goffman," he said. "And it's always better to sit than stand," he continued, gesturing that they should be seated. "You don't know anything about me, but I know quite a lot about you." Goffman eyed William seriously.

"Why am I here?" William blurted out.

"It's a long story, but it's for your own good. You'll learn more as time goes on. For right now you'll just have to trust me. Is that all right?" Goffman asked.

William studied him for a good while before nodding. "The video on the plane talked about candidates," he continued. "Am I a candidate?"

"I know things have been moving pretty fast today. You're mostly here because this is the safest place for you right now. But I also think you would make a good candidate. You'll find out more about that tomorrow," Goffman said with a secretive smile. "The classes here are quite out of the ordinary," he added.

"And where are my parents?"

"They're doing well and are out of danger at a secret location. But it was a close call this time."

"This time?" William asked.

"Yes. This isn't the first time Abraham Talley has tried."

Abraham Talley? William gulped. "Who is Abraham Talley?"

Goffman eyed him seriously. "A very . . . dangerous . . . man," he said quietly.

"Is he the reason we had to escape to Norway?" William asked.

Goffman hesitated a bit before answering. "In a way, yes."

"But why is he after us?" William asked.

Goffman leaned in even closer to William. "He's not after *us* at all. . . ." Goffman swallowed. "He's only after you."

William stiffened. "Just me?"

"But he won't get you here, William. The Institute is the absolute safest place you can be right now. Until we manage to track down Tobias."

William's heart skipped a beat. *Tobias?* "You mean—my grandfather?" William stammered.

"Yes, Tobias Wenton," Goffman said.

"You knew him?"

"Yes, I knew him well," Goffman continued. "He was one of the original founders of the Institute."

"What?" William shouted.

13

William jogged along next to Fritz Goffman, who was walking down the hallway with very long strides. He was still in shock and couldn't believe what he had just heard about his grandfather.

"Tobias Wenton was . . . *is* one of the best cryptologists in the world," Goffman said. "Do you know what a cryptologist is?"

"Someone who breaks codes," William responded.

"Exactly." Goffman smiled. "The Institute hasn't been the same since he disappeared."

"But . . . ," William began.

"I'm sure you have a lot of questions," Goffman interrupted. "And I'll answer them as best I can. But that will have to wait. It's late and we need some sleep. Your room is in the east wing, up the stairs. I think you'll be comfortable there."

William spotted the argu-bot. He expected it to hurl some comment or other at them, but it didn't. Instead it bowed politely as they went by.

"How long do I have to stay here?" William asked.

"As long as there is a risk that Abraham is trying to find you," Goffman said. "But I promise you: It won't be boring. We've tailored the coursework specially for people like you. You've come to the right place."

"People like me?" William said. "So I *am* a . . . candidate."

"We'll see. Since you'll be here with us for a while one way or the other, you might as well have something to work on," Goffman said with another sly smile, and continued on up the stairs.

The step bot was on its way down the middle of the stairs but stopped and scurried sideways to make room for Goffman and William.

They proceeded down a hallway to one of the big wings and came to a halt in front of a red door, which opened with a swoosh.

"The room isn't that big, but it has everything you'll need," Goffman said, showing William in. "You'll have a private lesson first thing tomorrow with Benjamin Slapperton. He'll explain more to you about what we do here at the Institute. He's a tad eccentric, but he's one of the best cryptologists we have, well, aside from your grandfather. Good night."

Goffman backed out of the room, and the door closed. William looked around. The room was sparsely furnished: a neatly made bed with a plaid comforter and pillow, a dresser, and a desk in front of a little window. William walked over to the bed and sat down. He thought about what Goffman had told him. Had his grandfather really been one of the Institute's founders? And what did they actually do here? And how could Goffman be so sure William would be safe?

William got up and went over to the door to make sure it was properly locked. He wiggled the handle.

"The doors are always locked after eleven p.m.," the door suddenly said. William jumped back in alarm.

"Huh?" William said. He leaned closer, noticing a little speaker right above the door handle. "You're a talking door?"

"This is just an entry-level position, a part-time job," the door said. "In a year or two, I'll have a completely different job. I have ambitions."

"Ambitions?" William repeated.

"Yes, ambitions," the door said firmly. "I'm a fabulous cook. I make the best lasagna in the world. No doubt about it. I'm going to have my own cooking show."

"How can you make lasagna when you don't have any arms?" William asked, taking a step back. After everything he'd seen at the Institute so far, he wouldn't be surprised if the door suddenly shot out a couple of bendy metal arms.

"Okay, you caught me. I'm just kidding. I'm a talking door. I had you fooled for a minute there, though," the door said with a hearty laugh.

William laughed too. He realized it felt good to laugh, so he laughed a little more.

"I know I don't have any right to ask about this," the door said a moment later, "but I get so curious when new people come to the Institute."

"What do you want to know?" William asked.

"Why are they bringing in a new candidate at this time of year?" the door asked.

"Maybe instead you could explain to me what a candidate is?" William said.

"They haven't told you that?" the door said.

"No."

The door paused for a moment. "Oh dear, I seem to have said too much. Again," it sighed.

"Come on. What's a candidate?" William asked.

The door paused again. "Okay. Candidates are code breakers . . . or people who are going to become code breakers, to be more precise. There, I said it. Don't ask me anything else," the door said.

"My grandfather was a code breaker," William said.

"Oh," said the door.

"I think he worked here at the Institute," William continued.

"What was his name?" the door asked.

William hesitated.

"Come on," the door said impatiently. "It takes two to have a conversation. I tell you something, then you tell me something."

William glanced around to make sure he was alone in the room. Then he leaned toward the door. "Tobias Wenton," he said.

It felt weird to say his grandfather's name out loud. When he was little, after he'd gone to bed, he would sometimes whisper it to himself under the covers. But he had never said it out loud. He looked at the door, waiting for a reaction, but it didn't make a sound. "Hello? Are you there?" William asked.

No response. William tapped lightly on the little speaker. "Are you there?"

"Tobias Wenton?" the door whispered. "Are you sure?"

"Yes, totally sure," William said. "Have you heard of him?"

"Have I heard of him?" the door whispered. "Tobias Wenton is the best cryptologist we've had here at the Institute. He actually lived in this room for years."

"He did?" William said, surprised.

"Yes, but he was away traveling a lot. I always looked forward to his coming back. He had so many funny stories. We were really good friends. And then suddenly . . ." The door faltered.

"He disappeared," William volunteered.

"Exactly. And he took with him . . ." The speaker crackled. "No, now I've said enough," the door said. "You'll have to talk to Mr. Goffman if you want to know more."

"Hold on!" William said. "What did he take with him?"

"Talk to Mr. Goffman," the door repeated. "Those two weren't exactly the best of friends before he disappeared . . . ," the door blurted out before going silent again.

"They weren't? Why not?" Now William really didn't want the conversation to end.

"I've said too much," the door said again, and then went silent.

William stood there for a while. Then he knocked cautiously on the door. "Hello?" he said, but the only response was the wind howling outside. William turned around and saw snow whipping against the little window.

He walked over and looked out into the darkness. He felt numb. Everything felt so unreal. Like a bad dream. Not that long ago he had been at home, back in Norway. Together with his parents. And now it felt like he'd suddenly been shot out from a large cannon and landed in this crazy place where he didn't know any of the rules. His mind was bubbling over with questions. Who was Abraham Talley? And why was Talley after him?

But he also felt closer to the truth than he had ever been for as long as he could remember. He turned and looked at the room. His grandfather had founded this place. William finally felt like he had a chance of finding him.

But why had he left the place that he had helped build?

"Knock knock..."

William grunted and pulled the blankets over his head. "KNOCK KNOCK!"

"Five more minutes, Mom," he mumbled. "Just five minutes!"

"I am not your mother," the door said, a little disconcerted.

Suddenly William remembered where he was. The plane trip, the Institute, Fritz Goffman, and the talking door. He sat up in bed, squinting with tired eyes into the sunlight shining through the little window and bathing the room in golden light.

"Knock knock," the door said again.

William looked at the clock. "Why are you nagging me like this? Don't you know how early it is?"

"You think I'm just doing this for my own enjoyment? There is actually someone knocking on me. KNOCK KNOCK KNOCK!" it called out again.

William swung his feet over the edge of the bed. "Who is it?" he asked the door.

"Who is it? Isn't that why people usually open doors? To find out who's on the other side?" the door said.

William got up and shuffled over the cold floor. He cautiously opened the door, stuck his head out, and looked around.

Not a soul.

Did he smell bacon?

"There's no one there," he said.

"Look down, dummy," the door teased.

On the floor there was a tray with fresh, steaming eggs, bacon, sausages, baked beans, buttered toast, and a cup of tea. William bent down and carefully picked up the tray in both hands. He backed into the room and shut the door with one foot. He set the tray on the desk and sat down.

"Is this synthetic, like on the plane?" he asked, glancing over at the door.

"Synthetic as all get-out, but just as good and much healthier," the door replied.

William stuck his fork into a thick slice of bacon and put it in his mouth. Then he tried the beans and eggs. They tasted great. Before he knew it, the plate was empty.

"That was one of the best breakfasts I've ever tasted!" he said, and took a good sip of the tea. William felt his energy starting to return.

He'd been so preoccupied with the delicious breakfast that he hadn't noticed the amazing view from the window. William set down the teacup, pushed the breakfast tray aside, and climbed up onto the desk. He pressed his nose to the cold glass.

Outside a snow-covered park stretched as far as he could see. Big trees that had to be several hundred years old, pruned bushes, statues, and fountains. In the middle of the park there was a frozen pond surrounded by benches and small gazebos.

William spotted a snow cloud moving behind a line of tall trees. An oval machine on treads came into view and proceeded across the garden. The machine looked like an enormous vacuum cleaner. A big, trumpetlike hose sucked in snow and then spit it out as dry snow crystals from a pipe on the top. The snow crystals sparkled in the sunlight before vanishing into thin air.

The oval machine passed a man who was rolling a big snowball ahead of him. The man had a red knit hat on his head and a big green scarf around his neck. He stopped at a snow fort and added the snowball to the end. Then he took a couple of steps back, put his hands proudly on his hips, and admired his creation. A small, square robot with a blue knit hat popped up behind the snow fort and nodded approvingly. Suddenly blue flames shot out of the man's feet, and he lifted off and flew over to the little robot. His hat fell off midflight. The sunlight gleamed off a shiny metallic head. He wasn't a man but a robot. William stared in fascination at the two robots as they continued making snowballs.

When the cloud of snow behind the oval machine was gone, William noticed a gigantic conservatory behind the trees. The conservatory must have been the size of a soccer stadium. William could just make out green shrubs and trees. Big red lamps shone down on the plants, and he could see the outlines of large, flying winged forms circling beneath the lamps. He tried to open his window to get a better view. But it was frozen shut and wouldn't budge.

"Knock . . . knock . . . KNOCK!"

William jumped in surprise and then hopped down off the desk. "Who is it?" he asked.

"KNOCK . . . KNOCK . . . KNOCK!" the door cried even louder. "Sorry. I'm programmed to adjust my volume to match the knocking on the outside. This must be Harriet. She's always in a hurry and knocks so hard I have a headache for hours afterward. Hurry up and open it before she knocks again."

William hurried over to the door and opened it. A small, rosy-cheeked woman in a gray skirt, lavender-colored blouse, and big eyeglasses stood before him. She was every bit as wide as she was tall and was holding a gray folder under her arm. She waved at William as she restlessly shuffled her high-heeled shoes back and forth.

"We're late. Come on!" she said before turning around and quickly walking away down the hall.

"Get going," the door said. "She doesn't wait." William put on his shoes and hurried out into the hall.

"Come on. We don't have all day!" the small woman called. She had already reached the end of the hallway, and William had to run to catch up to her.

"I'm Harriet, and I'm taking you to your orientation appointment with Benjamin Slapperton. Are you familiar with him?"

William shook his head. "No, I've only heard his name."

"He's a little odd," Harriet said, giving William a look over the top of her glasses. "But come on, now. We don't have much time."

They rounded a corner and continued down a narrow stone staircase. Harriet kept going without slowing her pace. Her short legs moved like drumsticks, and William had a hard time keeping up.

At the bottom of the stairs Harriet opened a heavy oak door, and they emerged from the back of the building. The morning sun shone from a cloudless sky, and the sounds of chirping birds could be heard. Harried kept moving through the snow-covered park William had seen from his room without slowing her pace. William glanced down at her high-heeled shoes, trudging along on the slippery footpath. He didn't understand how she managed not to fall.

Then he saw the gigantic conservatory he'd seen from his room. It towered over them like a mountain. Above a set of double wrought-iron doors hung a big sign that said:

CYBERNETIC GARDEN

DO NOT FEED THE PLANTS! (LEVEL 3)

"What is that?" William asked.

Harriet glanced up. "You'll find out soon enough."

"But what does 'level three' mean?" he continued.

"That means it'll be a while before they let you in there," she said, speeding up. "You can be glad about that. It's a dreadful place."

William glanced back at the sign as they hurried on. He knew what "cybernetic" meant. He'd read his grandfather's books on cybernetics. It was the science of advanced technical systems. Something you used when you built robots, for example. William looked over at the plants in the enormous conservatory. If a garden were cybernetic, that meant that it would somehow be synthetic.

William yearned to take a closer look, but that would have to wait. At the moment it was all he could do to keep up with the little racewalker ahead of him.

"Come on. We don't have all day," Harriet said, jogging

over the snow. William hurried after her but stopped when a snowball suddenly hit her on the back of the head. She howled and spun around.

"What are you doing?" she yelled, glaring at William as she brushed the snow out of her hair.

"It wasn't me," William said, scared.

"Nonsense, of course it was y—" she began but was interrupted by a new snowball, which hit her in the face, knocking her big eyeglasses right into the snow.

William turned in the direction the snowball had come from and spotted the two robots standing behind the wall of their snow fort a little way off.

"Someday I'm going to have you guys sent to the scrap heap," Harriet shouted, blowing snow off her glasses.

It didn't seem like they cared very much about her threats. The bigger of the two robots started making a fresh snowball.

"Hurry up!" Harriet yelled. "We're late."

They stopped outside a stone building with a domed copper roof. This building looked much older than the main building. A sign hung over the door saying ORBATORIUM in gilded letters. The door flew open, and a man in a white coat poked his head out.

"Good morning, Benjamin. I've brought William Wenton for orientation," Harriet said, nodding toward William.

Benjamin Slapperton held his hands up to shield his eyes from the bright sun. His hair was disheveled. He stood there looking at William for a moment.

Finally, his thoughts seeming far away, he said, "William Wenton?" and leaned forward.

Then he grabbed ahold of William's sweater and tugged

him through the doorway, the door slamming shut right in front of Harriet. William could hear her outside, complaining.

"Irritating woman," Slapperton said, looking at William. "Don't you think?"

William squirmed a bit. "I only just met her."

"Yes, that's right. You'll have to wait to get to know her before you start disliking her," Slapperton said, gesturing toward a chair in front of a big green chalkboard. "Have a seat."

William looked around. The room was round and the ceiling domed. The walls were lined with tall shelves filled with mechanical devices of various shapes and designs. A large brass steam engine stood in one corner, and a mechanical eagle hung from the ceiling. William quivered with excitement. Deep inside he knew this was more than just machinery. This room was full of mechanical codes, the kinds of codes he'd read about in his grandfather's books. Codes he'd never thought he would get to see in real life.

"You look like a completely normal kid," Slapperton said, sizing William up. "Imagine a kid who looks so ordinary being able to solve something as extraordinary as the Impossible Puzzle."

Slapperton scratched his dark mustache, which suddenly hopped down onto his shoulder.

"No, come back!" Slapperton yelled as he tried in vain

to catch the mustache, which moved down his jacket and then hopped over onto the desk. The mustache continued to zigzag through all the clutter. Slapperton upended a coffee cup, which he plopped down, capturing the mustache.

"Gotcha!" he yelled, beaming from ear to ear while he held the squirming mustache up for William to see.

"What do you think?" Slapperton asked contentedly. "I made it myself."

William hesitated. "What is it?"

"A mechanical mustache. It runs little errands for me and such. Very practical as long as it's behaving, but it can get a little cantankerous at times."

Slapperton put the mustache back on his upper lip.

"But what did I do with . . . hm . . . I mean, I just had it. . . ." Slapperton rummaged around on the desktop. "I put it right here. Ah, there it is," he said, picking up something that William immediately recognized.

"You've seen this before," Slapperton said, holding out a cylinder. It was the Impossible Puzzle.

"Yes." William blushed. "How did you get it?"

"I made it." Slapperton smiled proudly.

William sat up in the chair. "But . . . ," he began. Dozens of thoughts suddenly flooded his head. "Were you the ones who arranged the museum exhibit?"

"Yup," Slapperton said.

"But why?"

"To find you, of course," Slapperton said, looking at the metal cylinder. "We didn't know where in the world you were. So we sent the device out on a world tour. It took longer to find you than I thought it would. Norway, huh? Who'd have thought? But in the end you took the bait."

William was starting to feel scared. If his grandfather hadn't wanted the Institute to find them, maybe it wasn't such a good thing that he was here?

"I know what you're thinking," Slapperton said. "Why didn't your grandfather want us to find you?"

William looked up at Slapperton and nodded.

"Tobias was a tad paranoid before he disappeared, especially after your accident. He didn't want to take any chances and sent your family to a secret place. You inherited a lot from your grandfather, and I knew you wouldn't be able to keep yourself away." Slapperton smiled.

"But why?" William asked.

"Mostly because we think you're safer here," Slapperton said, and then cleared his throat. "And because I think you can help us find him."

"My grandfather?" William almost shouted.

"Yes," Slapperton said, setting the Impossible Puzzle down. He pulled something out of his jacket pocket. It was a sphere. He held it out so William could see. The sphere was the size of an apple, and it was covered with strange symbols.

"All of the candidates get one," Slapperton said, handing the sphere to William. It was cold and heavy. Much heavier than it looked.

There it was again: *the candidates.* William gave Slapperton a questioning look.

"I'm sorry. I forget that you don't know much about the Institute yet," Slapperton said. "The candidates are the next generation of code breakers, cryptographers in training. They all have special abilities that we're trying to develop here at the Institute. We found them almost the same way we found you, just not under such dramatic circumstances, of course."

"Did the other candidates win competitions too?" William asked.

"Yes. We have six other candidates here at the moment. The number varies, but there are never many. We're talking about extraordinarily talented people. And there aren't that many of those. You'll meet them tomorrow. Today you should spend your time familiarizing yourself with your orb." Slapperton pointed at the sphere sitting in William's hand.

"My orb? Is this an—ow!" William glanced down at the sphere and discovered a tiny needle, which had just pricked him. The needle disappeared back into the sphere.

"Nothing to worry about," Slapperton said. "It's just making sure you're the right person."

"The right person?" William repeated.

"Each orb is person specific. I'm sure you remember the samples that were taken when you arrived?"

William nodded.

"This orb has been specially programmed for you. It knows your genetic code, and you're the only one who can use it. And don't worry, it won't prick you every time you use it," Slapperton said, smiling wryly. "When you solve it to the first level it will do a full scan of you so that it can recognize you on sight."

"On sight?" William repeated.

"Yes. On sight. An orb is a key, but not just any old key. The orb is a mechanical puzzle that has ten levels. As you solve the levels, the orb takes on new properties. And you also gain access to new parts of the Institute," Slapperton said. "That's why it's imperative that only the owner can use his or her orb."

William remembered what it had said on the cybernetic-garden sign.

"So I have to get to level three before I can enter that enormous conservatory out there?" he asked.

"Correct. But you'll have to be patient. It usually takes a couple of weeks to solve the first level."

William glanced down at his orb. It had different parts that could be turned and twisted, just like the Impossible Puzzle. A glowing blue zero blinked on a little display.

"Does this mean I'm a candidate?" William asked.

"Would you like to be one?" Slapperton said.

William had to smile. This was almost too good to be true. "Yes," he said.

"Wonderful!" Slapperton said, clapping his hands. "But I have to go." He looked at the time and was suddenly in a hurry. "You can sit here and familiarize yourself with your orb. You'll find the way back on your own." Slapperton gathered up a stack of papers. "Just shut the door behind you when you leave. If you close the door all the way, it will lock automatically," he called, stumbling out.

William sat there by himself.

He closed his eyes and cautiously clasped his hands around the orb. He felt the familiar stirring in his stomach right away. A feeling of warmth spread up his spine and out to his arms. It was just him and the orb now. He opened his eyes again.

The symbols had started glowing, as if they had come free from the orb and were hovering in the air above it. Some of the symbols became smaller, while others grew and glowed brighter in different colors. And suddenly William detected a pattern. His fingers started twisting and turning the small pieces that held the orb together.

Then it started to vibrate.

The vibrations increased until it felt as if it would fall apart in his hands. William let go of the orb and gasped when it didn't fall but remained hovering in the air in front of him. Then the vibrations stopped. William stared at the metal sphere. Something inside the orb clicked a couple of times, and then it twisted a bit by itself as if it were looking around. A blue light shot out of a small hole in the metal. The beam of light hit William, visible as a glowing blue dot in the middle of his forehead, and then it started darting back and forth at lightning speed, as if it was scanning him.

The light traveled sideways up and down his body faster and faster until it started to form a shape. William looked down. It seemed like the light was shaping itself after his body. He took a step back and gasped as he could see himself standing in front of him. It was like the blue laser had made a hologram copy of him.

Then the hologram shrank and disappeared into the orb along with the light as quickly as it had appeared. The orb emitted a couple of electronic sounds before it suddenly moved toward William. It stopped right in front of him and floated there like it was waiting for something. William just stood there, unsure what to do. The orb moved even closer and poked him a couple of times in the chest. Then moved back again.

"You want me to hold you?" William whispered.

William reached out and carefully held his hand under the orb. The orb fell and landed perfectly in his palm. He felt the weight and looked at the little display. The zero had changed to a glowing number one.

William smiled. He had gotten to the first level. He turned the orb round in his hand and wondered if he could solve two more to get into the cybernetic garden.

He was dying to have a look.

16

An hour later William glanced down at the orb in his hand. A three was now blinking in the little display. Getting to each of the next two levels had been progressively more difficult than the first level. At level two the orb had grown to the size of a beach ball. And when William made it to level three, it shrank to the size of a marble. But he'd done it, and now he was standing in front of the iron door to the cybernetic garden.

William put his hand on the cold door and tried to pull it open, but it was locked. "I suppose this is where you come in," he said, holding up the little orb.

But what was he actually supposed to do? He remembered what Slapperton had said: The orb works like a key. He looked over the door. If the orb was a key, there had to be a keyhole somewhere, didn't there?

His eyes came to rest on a round hollow in the door. Inside the hollow he discovered a small, round brass sign. William leaned close to see better. A small orb and the number three were engraved in the brass. William raised his orb and held it in front of the hollow.

But nothing happened.

He moved it a little closer. Suddenly the orb was pulled out of his hand and hit the hollow with a loud bang.

Then it began to spin, and before William knew it, the door began to slide open. "Welcome to the Institute's cybernetic garden," a monotone voice said. "For security reasons, please remain on the marked paths and remember: Do not feed the plants. Have a pleasant visit."

"Thanks," William said, putting his orb in his pocket.

The garden was enormous, tall palms and lush trees for as far as he could see. He looked up. It must have been several hundred feet to the top, at least. Large birds circled overhead. It was like being in a jungle: hot, overpowering, and a little spooky.

A stone path led into the trees ahead of him. William started walking. After passing a small grove of trees, he emerged into something that looked like a park with large cages lining the path. William stopped in front of one of the cages and studied the green plant inside. It looked like a completely normal cactus. A little brass plate said FERRUM ICTUS.

"*Ferrum ictus . . . ,*" William said aloud to himself,

cautiously leaning closer. He knew that *ferrum* was Latin for "iron" and that *ictus* meant "bite": iron bite. Weird name for a cactus, he thought. And then it occurred to him that surely someone must have given the cactus that name for a reason. William pulled back just as the cactus lunged forward, a large mouth full of sharp steel teeth gaping. The cactus bit the metal bars as if it was trying to eat them.

"Wow!" William exclaimed, delighted. He stood there watching the cactus attacking its cage as if it was prey. Then it let go and hissed at William.

"A cybernetic robot cactus. Cool."

William turned to look at the other cages. Actually, most of the plants looked a little odd. Some of them even had little blinking lights here and there. William kept moving deeper into the garden, reading the names of the plants as he walked by: *Toxic vegetabilis, Pulchra inferno, Homicidum plantate, Diabolus infernum.*

William stopped by an enormous vine draped between two trees. It looked like a huge, green spiderweb. The plant was moving slowly back and forth as if it was swaying in the wind. But there wasn't any wind in here. William leaned forward and checked the sign: *Viridi polypus.*

"Green octopus," he said to himself.

He took a couple of steps back and stood, staring at the plant, as if he was expecting something to happen. Suddenly he heard a deafening scream overhead. He looked up and saw a gigantic bird diving toward him.

William was just about to throw himself to the ground when the vine shot into the air and grabbed the huge bird, wrapping it up in eight big tendrils. The bird screamed and flapped its enormous wings, but it was stuck tight. William stumbled backward without taking his eyes off the bird, which was struggling in vain against the greedy plant. The green octopus stuffed the desperate bird into its big, dark maw. After it chewed and swallowed, the plant emitted a loud burp, belching out feathers and metallic bone shards, which it spit on the ground.

William realized it was time to get out of there.

He looked around for an exit. He had been so preoccupied with all the plants that he had totally forgotten to keep track of the exact way he had come. He took his best guess and started walking back. Now all the plants seemed to be reaching for him with hungry, metallic jaws full of razor-sharp teeth.

He sped up.

A big sunflower turned toward him and growled. William jumped to the side and stumbled over a low fence that separated the path from a large lawn. A sign said KEEP OFF THE GRASS! in black letters. But he could see the wrought-iron door he had come in through on the far side of the grassy area. He looked around and then hopped over the fence and started running.

It took a few seconds before William realized he wasn't moving forward. He ran faster but still didn't budge. William looked down and saw that the grass was moving backward underneath him. Every single blade of grass was moving in the opposite direction from the way he wanted to go.

William stopped.

He was starting to panic. This wasn't normal grass. He turned around and began cautiously walking back toward the fence. But the grass just moved the other direction, and he stayed put, standing in the same spot. William looked around helplessly.

Then suddenly his feet flew out from underneath him, knocking the wind out of him when he hit the ground. He lay there, gasping for breath. He tried to get up, but no matter how hard he struggled, his arms and legs slid out to the sides.

Then the grass started moving in a specific direction. It was like he was being carried away by thousands of tiny ants. Suddenly he noticed a hole opening up in the middle of the lawn. It was gurgling and sloshing, and a terrible stench rose from the darkness behind big steel teeth.

"HELP!" William screamed at the top of his lungs.

He stared in horror as he came nearer and nearer to the big mouth. He closed his eyes and put his hands over his face. He was only seconds away from the steel teeth—then suddenly the grass stopped moving.

Am I dead? he thought. William didn't dare open his eyes. He just lay there, waiting for the grass to start moving again.

"If you wanted it switched off, you only had to ask!" a voice called from a little way away.

William opened his eyes and looked around. He was lying right next to the gaping hole. One of his pants legs was snagged on one of the metal teeth. The fabric ripped as he pulled his leg back. William got up and saw someone standing on the path on the far side of the fence.

It was a girl. She had dark hair pulled into a long braid that hung over one shoulder. She was holding a stack of books in her hands.

"All of the machines have off buttons. Look for it the next time you're about to be eaten," she said in all seriousness, pointing to a big red button on a control panel that said ON/OFF.

William ventured a smile. "Thank you."

The girl turned around and started to walk away.

"Wait!" William yelled, running after her.

She stopped and cocked her head at him.

William hopped over the low fence but stumbled and almost fell. He managed to regain his balance with a couple of unsteady steps.

"Thank you for . . . ," he began, glancing at the gaping hole in the lawn.

"Cibum tritor," she said wryly.

William gave her a questioning look.

"That means 'meat grinder.' Not particularly original, if you ask me. But of course originality is something most of these silly machines lack," she said, looking with disdain at the plants surrounding them.

"What's your name?" he asked.

"Iscia," she said matter-of-factly.

"Like that island off of Naples . . . in Italy?" William asked.

She nodded. "But without the *h*."

"Why were you named after an island?" William continued. There was something about this girl that made him curious.

She glanced quickly at the ground. "My parents were married there," she said, looking back up at him.

"Cool," he said. He had a lot more questions but decided to hold back.

"What is all this?" he asked, looking around the conservatory.

"Experiments, of course. Like the rest of the robots and doohickeys the Institute is stuffed full of," she said.

"I get the sense that you're not that fond of robots," William said. "Are you one of the candidates?"

"You sure ask a lot of questions," Iscia said. "How did you get in here anyway?"

"With this," William said, and pulled his orb out of his pocket.

"With that?" she exclaimed.

"Yes," William said.

"When did you get it?"

"Today."

"Have you solved your way to level three already?"

William blushed. He looked down and didn't say anything.

"Well, anyway, you don't have any reason to be here. I'm the only one who usually comes inside," Iscia said.

She turned and walked away with decisive steps. William stood there watching her until she disappeared behind two snarling rosebushes.

17

The next morning William hopped out of bed and shuffled
over the cold floor. He opened the door, expecting to find
a delicious breakfast like he had the day before, but he was
disappointed when the only thing outside his door was a
brown parcel.

"What are you waiting for?" the door asked. "Open it.
This is a big day."

William picked up the package and was even more disappointed to feel that it was soft. He walked over to the bed
and sat down. A little handwritten card had been stuck under
the tight twine. He pulled out the card and read: "Come to
the dining hall at exactly seven a.m."

William suddenly felt happy. Finally he would get to
meet the other candidates. And see Iscia again. He tore

open the package and looked at the contents.

A pile of clothes.

He stood up and laid the items out one by one on the bed: a gray tweed jacket, a light green shirt, a purple tie, a pair of dark blue pants, and a pair of black shoes.

A few minutes later he was standing in front of the mirror looking at himself. The jacket was a little big. And the pants were maybe a bit long.

He looked different. Too neat.

William messed up his hair. It didn't help.

He loosened the tie a little and opened the top button of the shirt. It didn't help either.

His eye fell on a leather patch stitched onto the outside of the chest pocket. He moved closer to the mirror and peered at it. It was a picture of an orb. He got his orb off the nightstand and slid it into the pocket. It fit perfectly.

"Good luck, William," the door said.

William walked toward the stairs. Something made him stop and turn around. An old woman stood at the end of the hall beside a janitor's cart. She looked at him without saying hello. A little hummingbird sat on her shoulder. William nodded to her before he turned and continued on his way. He cast one last look back before starting down the stairs, but the old woman was gone.

William paused in the doorway of the big dining hall. There had to be more than a hundred people in there.

Mostly grown-ups. A few in white lab coats, others in suits. Various robots scurried back and forth between the round tables. They were serving and clearing at a tremendous pace.

"William Wenton?" a voice asked.

William looked around and saw a tall, thin robot in a black suit rolling toward him on four little wheels.

"Yes," he replied.

"Follow me," the robot said, and then turned and headed back into the hall.

William gulped and followed, moving in between the tables. Some of the adults glanced up from their food and nodded. William nodded back. But most of them were too busy eating to notice him.

"William," he heard someone behind him say.

He turned around and saw Slapperton sitting alone at a table. Slapperton waved. "You'll be seeing me after breakfast. We'll talk then," he said with a smile.

William nodded briefly and kept following the wait-bot.

"Here you go. You will sit here." The robot pointed with a thin arm at a table where Iscia was sitting with five other people. Three boys and two other girls all looked up from their plates to stare at William.

They were wearing the same uniforms as him and looked to be about his age. William didn't think they looked particularly intelligent. In fact, they looked completely normal. They could've been in his class back home in Norway.

As he sat down, Iscia gave him a quick glance. He nodded to her, but she just kept eating.

Was she mad because of what had happened yesterday? Because he was at level three already? Or because he'd intruded on her turf? William shook his head. He had enough to worry about; she could have the garden to herself for all he cared.

18

"Just my luck," Slapperton moaned. "It won't budge."

He was standing on a stepladder using his pointer to thwack one of the rolled-up wall charts that hung over the whiteboard.

Each of the students—or candidates, as William now knew—was seated in his or her own chair, watching Slapperton impatiently. He straightened up on the stepladder, which wobbled precariously. Then he tugged hard on the handle of the wall chart, which suddenly came unstuck. The ladder tipped, and Slapperton fell backward, unrolling the chart as he went, and landed on his back on the desk. He leaped up, beaming triumphantly.

"You see? Anything is possible as long as you don't give up," he said contentedly, hopping down off the desk.

"Today is a bit of a special day, gang. We have a new candidate on the team. Let's welcome William Wenton." Slapperton pointed to William and smiled. "He's joining us all the way from Norway."

"Norway?" one of the other boys blurted out. Someone laughed.

"Do you have your orb with you?" Slapperton continued without addressing the teasing.

William nodded.

"Did you get anywhere with it yesterday?"

William hesitated. He glanced at the other candidates and then looked at the floor.

"I understand," Slapperton said. "Most people find the first level the most difficult."

William nodded vaguely.

"He's on level three," someone announced dryly from the back row. William peeked over his shoulder. It was Iscia.

A gasp went through the small group. Slapperton broke out into a violent coughing fit.

"Level three?" he asked, clearing his throat. "Let me see that!"

William pulled the orb from his chest pocket and held it out. Slapperton quickly snatched it, turned, and strode back to his desk. He mumbled something as he twisted and turned the orb, then scratched his head and stood with his back to the class. After he'd stood like that for what seemed like forever, he turned around and peered at William through narrowed eyes. William was sure there were going to be consequences. That he had broken some rule or other and that they were going to take the orb away from him or kick him out of the group.

"How did you manage to . . . ?" Slapperton pointed to the number three in the display.

William didn't respond.

Slapperton scanned the rest of the group.

"How many of you have reached level three?" he asked, holding up William's orb.

No one answered.

"How many?" he asked again. Iscia raised her hand.

"No one else?" Slapperton asked. "Freddy?"

Slapperton pointed to a big boy with curly brown hair. Freddy shook his head and gave William a dirty look.

"This is most extraordinary, William," Slapperton said, giving the orb back to him.

William quickly put the orb back into his pocket.

"We have many gifted candidates here at the Institute. But this . . . ," Slapperton continued, pulling a white remote control out of his pocket. He stood there staring at William for a moment before he shook off his surprise and decided to proceed.

"The history of technology, you guys, that's what we'll be learning more about today. How far did we get?"

William glanced around at the others. Freddy glared back at him. "Ancient Egyptian batteries," Iscia said.

"Ah, yes, ancient Egyptian batteries. And lamps that ran off electricity four and a half thousand years ago," Slapperton said, aiming the remote at the wall chart.

"And this is what they looked like," he continued as a picture of a clay vase appeared. "They were constructed the same way as modern batteries. Very simple, actually."

Slapperton pressed the remote control again. The clay vase disappeared, replaced by a basket of potatoes.

"How many potatoes does it take to light up a lightbulb?" he asked, looking out at the small class. "And, no, this isn't one of those how-many-people-does-it-take lightbulb jokes," he added with a smile.

Iscia raised her hand.

"Anyone else?" Slapperton asked.

"One," William said.

Iscia gave him a dirty look.

"Yup. There's enough electricity in one potato to light up a lightbulb," Slapperton said.

William had seen potato lamps like that before, in one of his grandfather's books. Slapperton stuck the remote control back into his pocket and moved around behind his desk. He picked up two boxes. One was full of potatoes and the other contained lightbulbs and wires.

"Now let's see if it works," Slapperton said, and looked

at the students. "Get up here and take whatever you think you need to get the lightbulbs going."

There was a quick rustle and scraping of chairs as the kids got up and went for the things on Slapperton's desk. William was the last in line, but he returned to his desk with a potato, a couple of copper leads, and a small lightbulb.

He put the potato on the desk and looked at the others who were already experimenting. None had gotten their bulbs to light yet. William knew that all he had to do was divide the potato into a positive and a negative section, insert the copper wires, and connect them to the lightbulb. Pretty simple actually. As long as you knew the principle.

A little more than a minute later William leaned back and looked at the white light coming from the little LED bulb.

"Wonderful, William," he heard Slapperton say. "Since you're done, maybe you could help the other kids."

William felt himself blushing. He had no desire to walk around and show the other kids anything at all. He looked around. A couple of the candidates glared at him. *Typical,* thought William. *I'm already becoming unpopular.*

"Hold on one second, William," Slapperton called when the class was over and everyone was leaving. "Could you wait for just a moment?"

William stopped in his tracks. Freddy bumped into him on his way out.

"Sorry," William said.

"Idiot," Freddy muttered.

"Close the door and come over here for a sec," Slapperton said. He followed William with his eyes, as if he wanted to tell him something. As if he was considering whether or not he should.

"I knew your grandfather really well," he finally said. William waited for him to go on.

"We were good friends right up until he disappeared. We went on digs all over the world together. Maybe I shouldn't tell you this. . . ." Slapperton hesitated.

"Tell me what?" William was feeling impatient.

Slapperton leaned closer and whispered, "Have you ever heard of luridium?"

Professor Slapperton walked over to a shelf full of test tubes. He put his index finger in one of the tubes and pushed it down an inch or so. Then he did the same thing with some of the other test tubes and took a step back. There was a restrained clinking as the shelf suddenly swung aside, revealing a dark passageway.

"Come. There's something I want to show you," Slapperton said, disappearing into the darkness.

The ceiling was just high enough for Slapperton to walk upright. William followed. "Where are we going?" he asked.

Slapperton pulled a little flashlight out of his jacket pocket and turned it on.

"Down here," he said, continuing down a couple of

narrow steps at the end of the passage. It smelled like old mold, and the walls were slippery with green algae. "The Institute is built on the foundation of an old castle," Slapperton said.

William shuddered. Dark, narrow passageways were not his thing. But if this would help him find out more about his grandfather, he would just have to clench his teeth and continue.

"We're almost there now," Slapperton whispered, stopping in front of an ancient door.

The door made a deep rumble as it swung open. Slapperton turned around toward William and gave him a serious look.

"You have to promise not to tell anyone about what you see in here. This is one of the best kept secrets at the Institute."

William nodded.

Slapperton turned around and went in. William hesitated.

"I can't turn on the light until you're in and we've shut the door," Slapperton said.

William stepped into the darkness and jumped as the heavy door banged shut behind him. He stood there waiting, fear oozing over him. Then he heard a soft click, and a light started flickering on the ceiling. William looked around. The room wasn't very big. The walls were brick.

Slapperton was standing next to something that looked like an old control panel. Otherwise the room was empty. Slapperton waved him over.

William had a sinking feeling in the pit of his stomach now. He was in a secret cellar beneath the Institute's foundations with a man he didn't actually know. And no one else knew he was here.

"You said you were going to show me something. What does this have to do with my grandfather?" William's voice sounded unsteady.

"Turn around for a second," Slapperton said.

As he did what Slapperton told him, William heard the squeaky sound of old metal buttons being pressed. Then Slapperton came and stood next to William. The floor beneath them started booming.

"Now you can see!" Slapperton whispered, pointing to the floor in the center of the room.

A round column slowly rose up out of the floor. The column had a diameter about the size of a manhole cover, and it stopped when it was as tall as Slapperton.

"Cool, huh?" Slapperton said, walking over to it. William followed.

An opening appeared in the middle of the stone cylinder. Behind the opening he saw thick glass.

"This is completely burglarproof. Even so, what used to be in there is gone now," Slapperton said.

A faint blue light, almost like a ghostly mist, pulsed behind the glass. William stood there entranced, staring at it.

"What is it?" William asked.

But Slapperton didn't answer. He just stood there, staring at the light pulsing behind the thick glass.

"Professor Slapperton?" William asked uncertainly. Slapperton snapped out of it.

"Luridium," he said. "Or . . . well, to be completely accurate . . . it *was* luridium. It's gone now. The light is the only thing left to prove it was there."

"Like radiation?" William asked.

"In a way," Slapperton said.

He gestured for William to take a closer look. William leaned forward and peered at the container behind the glass. It was empty.

"What's luridium?" he asked.

"Luridium is a kind of metal." Slapperton cleared his throat. "Or to be precise, intelligent metal—in other words a metal that can think for itself."

"Intelligent metal?" William repeated.

"It's composed of miniscule computers the size of atoms and can be programmed to change shape and turn into anything. It's like a smart, liquid computer program. It can take any form. Even a human brain," Slapperton said. A somber look came over his face. "Luridium is the most dangerous and most fascinating technology in the world. If it ends up in the wrong hands . . ." He paused. His eyes took on a vacant look. "But that's not the most amazing thing," he continued.

"What is then?" William asked.

"Luridium is very old and had been buried under thick layers of stone and coal for millions of years until a lump was discovered at the beginning of the 1860s."

William glanced up at Slapperton. "What happened?"

"That's when the work began digging the tunnels for the underground trains in London. One of the miners, a man named Abraham Talley, happened upon a lump of luridium while he was working on the first tunnel."

Abraham Talley, William thought. Fritz Goffman had mentioned him. He was the man who was after William.

"A terrible accident occurred right after the luridium was found," Slapperton continued. "Ten workers were killed. And Abraham was the only survivor. He was taken to the hospital, where he spent three days in a coma. By the time they figured out how the other workers had died, it was too late. Abraham had disappeared from the hospital without a trace."

"How did they die?" William asked.

"They were strangled. By Abraham." Slapperton paused, studying William as if checking to see that this wasn't too much for him.

"But why?" William asked.

"To cover up what he'd found. The luridium had already taken over his body. It was taking over his mind, too."

An impossible thought struck William. "But . . . if Abraham Talley discovered luridium over a hundred and fifty years ago, that would mean that—"

"He's very old, yes," Slapperton continued. "That's a side effect of having luridium in your body. Abraham vanished without a trace until he turned up again a hundred years later, in 1960. That was when your grandfather and a couple of colleagues founded the Institute, to keep the luridium from falling into the wrong hands. They started trying to find other sources of luridium as well. They hid what little they found here at the Institute, in this room, to keep Abraham from getting ahold of it."

"Abraham? But why did he come back?"

"To get more. He needs a refill," Slapperton said.

"Where is he now?" William asked.

"We don't know. He disappeared again eight years ago. Around the same time as your grandfather."

"Was he the one who attacked my family back home in Norway?" William was trembling.

"I don't think so. Probably one of his helpers," Slapperton said.

"But then Abraham managed to steal the luridium from

the Institute anyway?" William pointed to the empty container.

"Someone stole it, yes, but it wasn't Abraham," Slapperton said.

"Who was it then?" William asked.

"Your grandfather," Slapperton said.

By the time William finally reached the dining hall the next morning, the others were almost done eating. He took a plate and helped himself to breakfast from the buffet. He nodded at the other candidates before sitting down in his spot and wolfing down his food. He was starving.

He had hardly slept the previous night. It had been impossible to settle down after everything Slapperton had told him yesterday: about the luridium, Abraham Talley, and his grandfather. William couldn't believe that his grandfather had stolen from the Institute. He'd been thinking about it all night, and his head felt like it was filled with syrup. He needed to try to think about something else, so he looked around.

Iscia was sitting across from him, poking at her food

with her fork. He tried to catch her eye, but she was staring fixedly at her plate.

"Let me see your orb," a hoarse voice hissed from the other end of the table.

William looked up and saw Freddy glaring at him as he chewed with his mouth open. William took a bite of boiled egg and didn't respond. He didn't want any trouble.

But Freddy didn't back down.

"No newbie gets to level three on their orb in just one day, not without cheating," Freddy continued.

William tried to ignore him. He focused on his meal and slumped a little in his seat in an effort to make himself seem smaller. But this tactic didn't seem to have any effect on Freddy. He loaded his fork, and pulled back on it, aiming at William. A piece of bacon hit William right on the forehead and then flopped down into his lap.

"Leave him alone," Iscia snapped, without looking up.

"Shut up," Freddy said gruffly.

"I just want to eat in peace," Iscia said.

"Be quiet," Freddy said.

With a loud splat, half an egg hit her on the temple and fell onto her plate. Iscia clenched her fists and closed her eyes. William looked over at Freddy, who had a piece of sausage on his fork now. Freddy took aim at him again.

William lowered his gaze and kept eating.

"I suppose you think you're better than us just because

you had beginner's luck with your orb?" Freddy hissed.

"Keep it down over there!" one of the adults called.

William's forehead broke into a cold sweat, and adrenaline coursed through his veins. They sat there eating in silence for a bit. William lowered his shoulders and focused on his food. Suddenly the piece of sausage hit him square on the nose.

"Just ignore it," Iscia whispered. "He has the concentration of a goldfish, so he's bound to forget what he's doing soon."

William looked up and met Iscia's eyes. He felt a new strength growing within him as he looked at her.

"I said *shut up*!" Freddy was really angry now. A clump of scrambled eggs hit Iscia right on the eye. "No one here is interested in what you have to say," Freddy whispered, loading up his fork again.

"Cut it out," William said.

"Oh, hey, he *can* talk!" Freddy exclaimed snidely. William and Freddy stared at each other for a moment.

"Okay, two o'clock behind the Orbatorium. You're dead!" Freddy barked, and then got up and marched out.

It was two o'clock, and William was standing behind the Orbatorium, ready.

It didn't seem like they shoveled back here very often, because the snow came all the way up to his knees. But he didn't notice the cold; he was far too tense. He didn't usually end up in situations like this. Maybe it was because he hadn't slept well. Or because of what Slapperton had told him. He felt dazed and looked around. Maybe Freddy had gotten cold feet? Or had forgotten about the whole thing. William decided to wait a couple of minutes more. At least he could say that he had showed up. His fingers ached from the cold. He cupped his hands over his mouth and blew into them. It didn't help. They still trembled.

"Look at him." He suddenly heard Freddy's hoarse voice.

"Looks like a scared little bunny in the snow."

William turned around and saw Freddy and two of the other boys a little distance away.

"I'm ready," William blurted out. It was a lie, but what else could he say?

"You don't look ready," Freddy sneered. "You've never even been in an orb duel before, have you?" He snickered, holding up his orb.

An orb duel? William wondered. *What is Freddy talking about?* William had thought this was going to be a good old-fashioned fistfight. He was confused now.

Freddy's buddies moved away as Freddy took a firm hold of his orb with both hands and turned it a couple of times. He darted his eyes at William and moved a little closer before he stopped.

William hurriedly pulled his orb out of his jacket pocket. His heart was really pounding now. It felt like it was going to jump out of his chest. He had to get control over his hands.

Suddenly Freddy flung his orb at William. It shot forward at an insane speed.

William barely managed to fling himself down into the snow before the orb swooshed by, right over him. He rolled over and cautiously got to his knees, looking for Freddy's orb. But instead of crashing into the brick wall behind him, the orb curved around like a boomerang and came flying back. In a well-practiced motion, Freddy caught the orb like a professional baseball player. And before William could gather his wits, Freddy launched the orb at him again.

Once more William had to throw himself down into the cold snow. The orb returned to Freddy, and William got back up to his feet. He glanced around. He noted that the rest of the group had turned up as well, but he couldn't see Iscia anywhere. Everyone's attention was on him, watching in anticipation. From their expressions William got the impression that they had all shown up to see the new guy get it.

"What are you waiting for?" Freddy yelled. "Aren't *you* going to do anything? This is too easy."

William started fumbling with his own orb.

Suddenly Freddy's orb hit him in the stomach. It knocked him backward, and he hit the deep snow hard. He lay there on his back, his stomach throbbing from the impact. He struggled to breathe, feeling his lungs burn.

This was getting serious.

William glanced at Freddy's orb. It hovered right over him now. Like it was waiting for further instructions from Freddy. Suddenly it shot down at him with lightning speed and crashed into his chest. The pain was so intense that William couldn't even scream. He kicked at the orb, which hovered over him for a moment before it returned to Freddy. William grabbed his chest and tried to rub the pain away. He didn't know if he could take another blow now. He was losing.

William rolled over onto his stomach and lay there in the deep snow until he got control over his breath again. The cold snow soothed his chest, and he could feel himself getting calmer as the pain faded into the background.

He held his orb in his hands in front of him and concentrated. He could hear Freddy laughing.

"All you have to do is say 'surrender,' and I'll stop," Freddy shouted. "I promise."

William thought. Part of him wanted to just give up. He was cold, and his body felt like it had been trampled on by a herd of elephants. He stuck his head up and looked at the others. His eyes stopped at a figure standing behind the group. It was Iscia. She lifted her hand and held up four fingers. William immediately knew what she meant.

It was like a burst of energy shot through him. And he knew that he couldn't give up. Not now.

"What do you say?" shouted Freddy. "You give up?"

"No," said William through clenched teeth. He looked down at his own orb.

"What?" said Freddy.

But William didn't answer. He was already starting to focus intently. He had made up his mind. He was not going to give up without a fight. And he had to solve the orb to level four before he could fight Freddy. Just like Iscia had showed him.

He focused.

It started in his stomach and spread to his arms and his head. And then his fingers started working. He could feel something whooshing by over his head. It was probably Freddy's orb again. But he didn't care. All his attention was on his own orb now, which clicked a few times, and a glowing four appeared on the display. He had reached another level.

William looked up and saw Freddy throwing his orb toward him again. William rolled around and tossed his orb up into the air. A bright light shot out of it and formed a see-through wall in front of him. Freddy's orb smashed into the glowing shield and bounced back toward Freddy.

A gasp went through the small crowd as the orb hit Freddy in the stomach so hard he fell backward into the snow. The orb stopped over him and hovered there. One of the boys tried to help Freddy, but he tore loose from his grip.

"Let go," he sneered as he got up.

Meanwhile, William had gotten to his feet and stood there waiting. He looked at the others. Their expressions had changed now. It was like they didn't understand what was going on. He looked at Iscia.

"Watch out," she cried.

Freddy's orb was headed toward him again.

William jumped to the side and threw his orb into the air. The glowing wall appeared again and a loud zap was heard as Freddy's orb crashed into it. But this time it didn't bounce back. It seemed to be stuck in the wall. It smoked and hummed before it exploded into hundreds of smaller pieces that scattered in the snow.

William looked at his own orb, which was still hovering above him. The bright light disappeared. He held out his hand, and the orb dropped into his palm.

He looked up at Freddy staring back at him, speechless.

"B-b-but how . . . ?" he stuttered. His face was almost as white as the snow. His buddies pulled him away, and they disappeared around the corner of the building.

William's eyes searched for Iscia. But she was gone.

Big snowflakes wafted down over the large open area behind the Institute. William shivered as he walked. Rows of majestic trees towered over him on both sides of the footpath.

He glanced down at the orb in his hand. He was on level four now. It was as if his orb had understood that he needed help, he thought. Or as if he and the orb had helped each other. He tucked the orb well down into his jacket pocket as he wondered what other secrets the little sphere might be hiding.

William stopped. He suddenly felt like someone was

staring at him. He looked up and spotted Iscia standing under one of the big trees.

"William," she called, waving him over.

As he approached, she pulled herself all the way in against the trunk of the big tree and gestured that he should follow suit. The long, snow-covered branches hung over them and hid them completely from the windows in the building ahead of them.

"Thanks," she said.

"What for?" William asked, a little surprised.

"For putting Freddy in his place. He had that coming."

"I think I wrecked his orb," William said. He felt a little guilty about that.

"Relax," Iscia snorted. "It'll be repaired. In a worst-case scenario, he'll get a new one. Then he'd have to start all over again from scratch." Iscia smiled with a wry glint in her eye.

Then she held out her hand to him. "Friends?"

William stared at her hand as if it were a creature from another planet. "Friends?" she repeated.

He took her hand. It was warm. "Friends," he said, and smiled.

William slept like a rock the whole night, and when he woke
up, his feelings of guilt at destroying Freddy's orb were gone.
Freddy ignored him all through breakfast. *Sometimes it's good
to fight fire with fire,* William thought. When breakfast was
over, they were given their schedule for the day. The first
item on the agenda was cosmological problem solving with
Professor Maple.

The big oak door of the Cosmotorium slid open, and
an old, stooped woman in a striped dress hobbled in, supporting herself on a cane. She was the oldest professor at
the Institute and moved like a tortoise. Iscia had warned
William at breakfast.

"Take your seats!" Professor Maple called in a crackly voice.

William followed her with his eyes. She stopped in front

of the stairs that led up to the small podium where her desk was located.

"Do you think she's going to make it?" he whispered.

"Wait and see," Iscia responded, right behind him.

All the students moved to their places and waited. Professor Maple stood still for a bit, then she clapped loudly and raised her arms out to the sides as if she were planning to fly up the stairs. Suddenly two robot arms dropped down from the ceiling. As if the old woman were a little toddler, the robot arms picked her up and stopped above the chair behind the desk on the podium. The robot arms turned her around, set her down on the chair, and then vanished just as quickly as they had appeared.

"Well, what are you waiting for? Sit down!" Professor Maple called, waving her cane.

William sat down and looked around. The ceiling was painted with stars and planets. Tall shelves filled with globes lined the walls. Some of the globes were as small as apples while others were the size of beach balls.

"We'll pick up where we left off last week," Professor Maple announced, pressing a button on her desk.

A small, square box with three small lenses hummed above her. A light flared up in the lenses and then disappeared.

"Darned projector! Haven't they looked at it yet?" grunted the professor, raising her cane.

She whacked the machine a couple of times. The light

came on again, and she lowered her cane. Suddenly the little projector fell off the ceiling and lurched toward the old woman.

"Watch out!" William called before he had a chance to reconsider.

But instead of crashing into her head, the projector veered to the side and continued into the room. It spun around a couple of times before swooping down toward the floor and then up into the air again.

"Quit showing off," the professor chided, rapping on her desk.

The projector composed itself and settled calmly in the air above them. William stared at the little box in fascination. It hummed faintly, hovering overhead.

The light came back on in the lenses, and a 3-D sphere appeared in midair in front of them. The hovering sphere grew in both size and brightness until it was as big as a basketball. Then it began to rotate. William thought it looked like a small, burning sun. Then a new planet appeared next to the burning sun. The new planet was smaller and gray with dark spots. It started orbiting the larger one. *Mercury,* William thought.

One planet after another appeared and began orbiting, and William realized that he was looking at the solar system with the sun in the middle. Then the solar system shrank in scale, and stars appeared.

William had read some of his grandfather's astronomy books. He looked up at the galaxy slowly rotating above them and thought that the earth wasn't actually all that big. And that if his grandfather was somewhere on such a small planet, William ought to be able to find him.

"Get started," Professor Maple called, snapping William out of his daydream.

He looked up and saw the planets and stars heading toward him. The galaxy multiplied, one descending to hover in front of each candidate.

"You have one hour to re-create the Milky Way," Professor Maple said before pressing another button on her desk. A screen appeared in front of her.

"And now we'll make some wonderful chocolate cupcakes as easy as one two three," a silken voice announced from her monitor.

William sat on a bench out in the garden eating the lunch he had made for himself in the cafeteria that morning. The rest of the candidates were sitting with Freddy a little way away. Every once in a while Freddy would whisper something and point at William. The others in the group would snicker and chuckle.

"They're a bunch of fools," a voice behind William said. He looked up.

Iscia sat down next to him.

"They couldn't find south if they were at the North Pole," she continued. "I noticed you finished your galaxy. Why didn't you say anything to Professor Maple? You could have scored some bonus points with her."

"I don't know," William said, looking down at his lunch.

After having lived for so long in hiding, he wasn't used to letting people see that he was good at things. Nor had he ever really felt the need to prove anything. But with Iscia it was different. He wanted to show her what he could do. He was glad she'd noticed that he had finished early.

"Look over there," Iscia said, pointing at Professor Maple, who was coming out of the Cosmotorium. She locked the door behind her, put the key in her pocket, and then shuffled away across the open area, supporting herself on her cane. She was holding a stack of gray folders under her arm. Iscia kept her eyes on the folders as Professor Maple passed them.

"Do you see those folders?" Iscia whispered.

"Mmm," William said.

"I wish I knew what was in them!"

"What are they for?" William asked, getting up.

"I don't really know. But they're always writing in them. I'm guessing, but I think they contain information about us. I've asked to see my folder a bunch of times. But they just say no. I think the Institute actually knows more about us than we do." She stood up, brushing the snow off the seat of her pants.

"But I'd really like to know where they're planning to send me. I'm sure that's in the folder," she said thoughtfully.

"Send you?" William asked.

"Every year some of the candidates are sent away. I don't know why. Everything is kept secret. Not even the ones going know where they're headed."

"You're kidding, right?" William said. But Iscia just looked even more serious.

"No, I'm not kidding. And I have a feeling that it won't be long before I'm sent away," she said.

"And you think that's in your folder?"

"I'm not totally sure. I hope so," Iscia said.

"Where do they keep the folders when they're not in use?" William asked.

Iscia shook her head. "I've heard they lock them in a room they call the Archive. But I don't know where it is. I've only heard rumors. I don't even know if there is an Archive."

William thought about this, a secret archive full of information. That was exactly what he needed now. Based on what Slapperton had told him, he was convinced that the Institute had answers about where his grandfather was and why he'd run off with the luridium.

"We need a map or a floor plan," William said, scratching his scalp.

"The projector!" Iscia said suddenly.

"What do you mean?"

"Professor Maple's projector has maps and holographic models of pretty much everything. Maybe it has something for the Institute?"

"Then we'll borrow it for a bit," William said, pulling Iscia along behind him toward the Cosmotorium.

The Cosmotorium door swung open silently, and William
peeked into the dark room. The projector was still hanging
from the ceiling over Professor Maple's desk. William slipped
in and waved to Iscia. She stuck her head in and looked
around skeptically.

"I don't like this," she whispered.

"It'll be fine. Come on," William said, handing her a
bobby pin.

"How did you learn to pick locks?" she asked, sticking
the pin back in her hair.

"I read about it in a book," he said.

Iscia looked up at the projector. "If we get it down, we
have to take it somewhere else. There's a guard here," she
said, peering around nervously.

"We have to get it down first," William said, stopping next to the teacher's big desk.

He spotted a button in the right-hand corner. He pushed it. The projector started humming, but it didn't move.

"Why's it just hovering there? We need to get it to come down!"

William looked around. Then he had an idea. He pointed to the two arms hanging from the ceiling right over the whiteboard behind the desk.

"We just have to clap, right?"

He clapped twice. The robot arms twitched before coming to life and running along a track in the ceiling. They stopped right above them and picked Iscia up.

"Not me!" she wailed.

But it was too late. Soon she was suspended, dangling in the air above William.

"Sorry," William said. "I thought they would take me. See if you can grab the projector since you're up there." William hid a small smile.

"I'm really not a fan of heights," Iscia sighed.

"Do you want to get into the Archive or not?"

Iscia closed her eyes. It looked like she was counting in her head. When she opened her eyes again, she was calmer.

"Okay, take me to the projector," she announced loudly and clearly to the strong metal arms holding her.

The arms transported her across the room, stopping right

in front of the projector. "Try to get it down," William said.

Iscia cautiously took hold of the little projector and pulled it down. She held it in front of her, her arms outstretched, as if it were a stinky old sock.

"Set me down again," she said without taking her eyes off the projector. The arms twitched again and transported her back, setting her down next to William.

"We have to get out of here before somebody notices us," she said, handing him the projector.

William and Iscia were soon walking rapidly through the large park behind the Institute. Iscia kept glancing around as if she expected someone to discover them at any moment. William held both of his hands over a bulge under his jacket.

"We have to find a place where we can work without anyone seeing us," William said.

"In here," Iscia said, pulling him toward the cybernetic garden.

William resisted. "What about the man-eating plants?"

"Just do as I say and you'll be safe," Iscia said. "I just let a set of mechanical arms fling me around. I'm sure you can deal with a little greenhouse."

"Greenhouse, huh?" William said, eyeing the conservatory structure towering over them.

They stopped in front of the enormous iron door that led into the garden.

William had absolutely no desire to go in there, not after what had happened the last time, but he was just going to have to trust Iscia. Right now, his need to find out more about his grandfather trumped his fear of the plants.

Iscia pulled her orb out of her jacket pocket and placed it in the hollow spot in the middle of the door. The heavy iron door soon swung open.

"Are you coming?" she said, looking at him.

William stood there, staring at the seemingly harmless grassy lawn a little way in.

"The grass is safe as long as you don't step on it," Iscia said. "And the most dangerous plants are in their cages. Just don't get too close to them."

William took a deep breath, lowered his shoulders, and exhaled. It helped. He felt a little calmer.

He followed Iscia in among the tall trees and perilous plants. Some of them bared their teeth at them as they passed. Others turned away as if they weren't interested.

"Looks like they were just fed," Iscia said, pointing to a plant that was lying down with its mouth wide open, snoring. "That's good. I usually come here to read. Nobody bothers me." Iscia turned onto a narrower path.

William jogged to catch up. They followed the winding path deeper into the gigantic greenhouse until they came to a large hedge. There was a door in the middle of the hedge. Iscia opened it and went in with William close behind her.

There were no bars and no plants snapping at them in here, just a big, open space. Three benches sat around a fountain with a statue of a woman in the middle. She was holding a big copper clock over her head.

"Aren't they cute?" Iscia said, pointing down into the water.

William stopped next to her. He could see big, colorful fish gliding by beneath the surface of the water. One of the fish stuck its head out of the water and looked at them.

"They like it when you pet them," Iscia said.

"Are you sure?"

"Yeah. Pat them on the head."

William leaned over and reached his hand out. He was about to touch one of the fish when it suddenly spit out a long stream of water that hit him in the face. William leaped back, spluttering. Iscia laughed so hard she had to sit down on one of the benches.

"That wasn't funny," William mumbled.

"Are you kidding? It was hilarious," Iscia hiccupped, wiping away tears. They sat there for a bit without saying anything.

"It's very quiet in here," William said.

"Yes, very."

Iscia suddenly grew serious, turned to face William, and pointed at the lump in his jacket. "Let's get this over with," she said.

William carefully stuck his hand into his jacket and pulled out the projector.

"Maybe it has an on/off button," he said, turning it over.

"Professor Maple usually bangs on it when it acts up," Iscia said.

"Then that's what we'll do." William rapped on it a couple of times, but nothing happened.

William tried again, harder this time. Still nothing.

"Maybe there's some other way to find out where the Archive is," Iscia suggested. "Let's just take this back and try something else."

"Maybe you're right. The projector's probably broken," William said.

He was about to stand up when Iscia cried, "Look . . . a light!"

She was pointing at the lenses.

Then the projector started humming. And before William had a chance to react, it shot up into the air. He was so startled he forgot to let go. The projector pulled him up. It stopped when it was dangerously high, with William dangling underneath. He glanced at Iscia, standing way down below, scurrying back and forth.

"Let go!" she called. "Aim for the fountain. I'm sure it's deep enough!"

William shook his head and closed his eyes.

"It's trying to shake you off!" he heard Iscia yelling.

BOBBIE PEERS

William clung on as hard as he could. Suddenly the projector dove downward. William opened his eyes as they struck a big rosebush. Branches with sharp thorns jabbed him all over. Then the projector did a U-turn and swooped back up again and over the hedge into the main part of the greenhouse. Once there, it started dive-bombing all the cages and stopped right above a plant William recognized immediately. It was the green octopus vine that had caught that big bird the last time he was here. The long, green tentacles started twisting up toward him. William shook the projector.

"Get us away. It's going to eat us both!"

But the projector didn't budge. William looked down again. One of the tentacles was just beneath him now. It was reaching for his feet. There was a click inside the projector, and the lights in the lenses went out. Then they started losing height.

"No, not now!" William cried.

He looked down and saw that Iscia had stopped right outside the plant's cage. She was looking up at him, her eyes wide with horror.

"Do something!" he cried.

"Like what?" she yelled back, looking around panic-stricken.

"Anything!"

The first tentacle got hold of one of his legs and started tightening. "I'm going to burst!" William screamed.

The green tentacle pulled him down farther. One of the other tentacles twined around his hips and tightened. The projector hummed to life again and started pulling upward, but one of the tentacles grabbed it and pulled it down. Soon green tentacles surrounded William and the projector, grasping and curling around them.

William stopped struggling.

He looked down at a dark mouth in the ground, remembering how the big bird had been chewed to bits and spit out again. In a few seconds the same thing was going to happen to him.

Suddenly he remembered his orb. He maneuvered it out of his pocket. "Can you help me?" he whispered.

One of the tentacles instantly shot up and thwacked the orb out of his hand. "No!" William cried as his orb fell into the dark mouth beneath him.

Then everything went completely still. The tentacles stopped moving. William hung there, waiting. Sweat poured down his face, and his heart was hammering so hard it felt like it would pound right through his rib cage.

"What's going on?" Iscia yelled from somewhere on the other side of the green tentacles.

The plant started coughing and clearing its throat, and suddenly the dark mouth spit out the orb. It hung there in the air in front of William.

"Are you going to help me or not?" William asked, and

looked at the orb like he expected it to suddenly talk back at him.

But the orb just continued to hover. William could feel the tentacles tighten round his chest. Soon he wouldn't be able to breathe at all. In sheer desperation, he grabbed the orb and started beating at the tentacle round his chest.

Suddenly William felt that tentacle loosen its grip. He was finally able to inhale, filling his lungs with air. He could feel his strength returning together with the fresh oxygen. He looked down at the huge plant. It seemed like it could feel pain.

"Do it more," he heard Iscia call out.

William kept beating at the vine. For every blow he could feel the green tentacle letting go. More and more. He kept hammering desperately until he suddenly dropped to the ground, landing right next to the gaping mouth. The projector bounced off a huge leaf next to him. He managed to grab it before it tumbled into the darkness.

William and Iscia were back on the bench again shortly thereafter. Apart from a couple of scrapes on his forehead and several rips in his jacket, he had emerged from the drama unharmed.

"Remind me, would you, not to come in here with you ever again," William said.

Iscia smiled and poked him in the side with her elbow.

"But you won! You conquered one of the most dangerous plants they have in here."

"Doesn't matter. I've already used up all my chances in this garden," William said.

"I think it likes you now," Iscia said, looking at the projector, which was hovering next to William. It was rubbing against his shoulder and purring like a cat.

"Maybe it just needs to be tamed?"

"Maybe," Iscia said.

"We need a map of the Institute," William said, looking expectantly at the projector.

The projector pulled away and hung there in the air as if it were contemplating what William had just said. Suddenly a hologram of the Milky Way appeared in front of them.

"No, not the Milky Way—the Institute," William said.

The hologram of the Milky Way disappeared, replaced by a map of London.

Iscia leaned toward the projector. "The Institute!" she said enunciating loudly and clearly.

A new image appeared in front of them, an architectural drawing. "Gotcha!" Iscia cried.

They sat there looking at the drawing hovering in the air in front of them.

"Wow, look at all those rooms," Iscia exclaimed. "This place is a lot bigger than I thought."

She pointed to the text at the top of the map.

Institute for Post-Human Research

Founded 1967

"Here's the main building," William said.

"And there's Goffman's office," Iscia said.

"But what's that right there?" William asked, pointing to a big unlabeled area behind the office.

"It doesn't say," Iscia said.

"Could that be the Archive?"

"If it is, we might as well forget the whole thing," she said in disappointment. "No one enters Goffman's office without permission."

They sat there in silence for a while.

"We'll do it tonight," William finally said, nodding his head decisively.

"Are you crazy?" Iscia asked.

"I thought you wanted to know what it says in your folder?"

"Yeah," she said, dragging the word out.

"And I need to find out about my grandfather. I think they know more than they're telling me," William said.

"About your grandfather?" Iscia said.

William didn't respond. He just sat there looking at her. Finally he said, "Do you know what luridium is?"

"Luridium?" she repeated.

"Yes," William said. "Have you heard of it?"

Iscia shook her head. "Never. What a weird name. What is it?"

"I'll tell you more tonight," he said, getting up. "Let's meet in the dining hall at ten p.m."

Iscia remained seated. The idea of breaking into Goffman's office clearly scared her.

But William knew he couldn't stop now. Not when they were so close to finding a whole Archive full of secret information.

24

It was 10:12 p.m. William crept down the stairs to the first floor as quickly as he could. He was late because his door had suddenly refused to let him out. It had lectured him all about how it was too late to go out and how it wasn't safe to run around the Institute at night. You never knew what you might run into. William had to use all his persuasive abilities before the door eventually, grudgingly let him out. Now he just hoped Iscia hadn't gotten cold feet.

William stopped when he reached the bottom step and listened. Darkness lay like a black fog over the big hallway. He was alone. A solitary wall lamp gave off just enough light for William to see where to go.

William continued down the hallway, which led to the dining hall. He stopped next to a metal statue that resembled the Statue of Liberty and peered around.

"Iscia," he whispered.

The only thing he heard in response was a faint echo of his own voice. Iscia had probably been here and left again when he hadn't shown up at the appointed time. William wondered whether he ought to just go back to his room too.

A creaking sound made him turn around. A silhouette was moving along the hallway. Holding his breath, William squeezed in between the wall and the statue.

The silhouette was coming closer. It was the same old woman he'd seen before in the hallway outside his room. She was pushing a cart full of buckets, brooms, and rags in front of her. William pressed himself against the wall. No one could know he was out wandering the hallways at this hour. The woman stopped right next to the statue and looked around. He could see her very clearly now. She was very old. Her skin was gray and wrinkled, and she wore her hair up in a little hair net. A small, mechanical hummingbird sat on her shoulder grooming its feathers. She looked around, then kept moving along the hallway, finally disappearing around a corner.

William didn't dare come out from behind the statue until the sound of the cleaning cart's squeaking wheels was completely gone. If Iscia didn't show up . . . should he try to find the Archive alone? No, he needed Iscia. She knew the Institute much better than he did.

"Psst," he suddenly heard from somewhere in the darkness. William stopped.

"Here . . . up the stairs."

William saw a narrow staircase a little way down the hallway. It was blocked with a chain, and there was a brass sign hanging from the chain that said EMPLOYEES ONLY.

"Hurry up," the voice whispered again. It was Iscia.

She was sitting halfway up the stairs, hiding. William stepped over the chain and climbed up to her.

"You're late."

"I was negotiating a curfew with my door," William explained.

"So what time does the little one need to be back, then?" she said sarcastically.

"Forget it," William said, and continued up the staircase.

Soon they were on the second floor, peering down a long, white hallway that seemed to go on forever.

"You lead the way. I've never been to Goffman's office," William said.

The hallway was so blindingly white that it was hard to see where the floor ended and the walls began. William ran his hand along the smooth wall to keep a straight course.

They went around a corner and stopped. "There it is," Iscia said.

In front of them there was a white door with no knob or handle. It almost blended into the wall.

"How do we get in?" William asked.

"No idea," Iscia responded. "You're the genius here."

William walked over to the door. He ran his hand over its smooth surface. He stopped for a second and almost had to smile. "Could it be so easy?" he mumbled.

"What are you talking about?" Iscia said.

William put one hand on the surface.

"The new fridge we got last year had no handle," William said, pushing in on the door.

The door made a click and swung open.

"Things aren't always so complicated," he said with a smile.

"But why doesn't Goffman's door have a lock?" Iscia asked skeptically.

"Don't know. Maybe because he's the boss, and he doesn't think anyone would dare to break in to his office," William said, peering cautiously around. "Come on!"

Goffman's office was nearly empty. A big, white desk sat in the middle of the room. There was an old globe on it.

"I can't see any door into the Archive," Iscia said.

"Don't give up so quickly," William said, moving farther into the room.

He stopped when he felt the familiar vibration in his body. It started in the pit of his stomach. He lowered his shoulders and closed his eyes.

"Um, what are you doing?" Iscia asked.

"Shh," he said, concentrating on the darkness under his eyelids.

He felt the vibrations increasing. Soon they were traveling up his spine and out to his arms and head. When he opened his eyes again, he saw it immediately: glowing symbols hovering in the air over the globe. Some were bigger than others and glowing more brightly.

"Do you see anything?" he heard Iscia ask. She sounded far away.

One of the symbols was glowing much brighter than the others. So was an X which had settled on top of what must be north on the globe. William spun the globe so the glowing symbol was directly over the X. He heard a click. The symbol disappeared, and a new one appeared. He did the same thing again. Another distant click.

"What's going on?" Iscia asked, leaning on the desk.

And now William felt it too. The whole office was vibrating.

"I don't like this," Iscia whispered.

"We're moving," William said, staring at a ballpoint pen rolling across the desk. "The whole room is moving."

"Like an elevator?" Iscia asked.

And just as quickly as the vibrations had begun, they stopped. William and Iscia stood there, listening, but nothing happened.

"What do we do now?" she whispered, moving closer to him. William surveyed the room.

"Could it be . . . ," he muttered to himself, and walked toward the door.

He put his hand on the cold surface and pushed carefully. The door swung open, and Iscia gasped.

They were staring into pitch darkness on the other side of the door. A cool draft hit them.

William took a step toward the doorway and stopped. "Careful," Iscia said. "I've heard so many stories. . . ."

William knew that he had no choice. If he was going to find out more about his grandfather, there was only one thing to do. He walked into the darkness. He heard a faint humming way up ahead, otherwise it was completely quiet.

"We're in this together," Iscia said, shutting the door behind them. William smiled.

Suddenly they began to hear clicking above them, and soon hundreds of lightbulbs started blinking on. It was like fireworks before the clicking subsided and they got used to the light.

"Wow," Iscia exclaimed, rubbing her eyes.

A vast, white room revealed itself before them. The ceiling must have been sixty feet high. And the space was filled with endless rows of archival shelves that towered over them.

The ceiling was covered with small vents, and a display on the wall next to them showed the humidity. It was very low.

"What if what we're looking for is way up there?" Iscia asked, pointing up the shelves.

"There must be some way of getting up there," William said, peering around. His eyes stopped at a sign that hung from the closest archive shelf. *Beware of Laika* it said in big, handwritten letters. "Who's Laika?" He glanced at Iscia.

"Beats me, but I don't like it. . . ." She went quiet. "Shh," she whispered.

They stood listening.

"There it is again," she whispered.

And now William heard it too—a faint echo of something moving somewhere in the stacks.

"It's getting closer," he said, taking a few steps backward.

Suddenly two stepladders on wheels came zipping out from behind one of the shelves, one was black and the other gray. Each one had a platform on top of something that looked like an upright accordion. William immediately made the connection. It was obvious—these were used for getting up to the higher parts of the tall shelves.

The stepladders came rolling toward them at a crazy speed. It almost seemed like they were racing each other. The black stepladder tried to cut the other one off, trying to push it into one of the shelves. They swerved on screeching tires the last little way and stopped right in front of William and Iscia.

"Pick me!" the stepladders cried in unison. "Pick me!"

"Wait a second," the black stepladder said. "There's two of them."

"Two of them?" the gray one said.

"Yes, two of them," the black one said.

The stepladders were quiet, as if this was information they had to contemplate for a moment.

"Pick me!" the black one said.

"No, pick me," the gray one said.

"Pick me!" they yelled in unison.

"What kind of bots are you?" William asked.

"We're stepbrothers," one of the stepladders blurted out.

"No, we're not," the other said. "We're in no way related."

"What are you then?" said William impatiently.

"Vertical bots," the stepladders said in unison. "We'll drive you wherever you want, whenever you want, and however high you want."

"Perfect. We'll take one each," William said, glancing at Iscia.

"Pick me! Pick me!" the stepladders yelled in unison.

Iscia hesitated.

William hopped up onto the black stepladder. "Come on. It'll be fun," he said, looking down at Iscia.

She rolled her eyes and climbed up onto the first rung of the gray stepladder.

"Where to?" the stepladders yelled in unison.

William smiled. He thought the ladders were funny. They seemed completely desperate to be of use. Maybe they were starved for company? No doubt it was terribly lonely here in the enormous Archive.

"Iscia would like her folder, and I would like to know more about Tobias Wenton," William said.

"Ugh, boring. We have a lot of material in here that's way more fun than that," said the stepladder William was standing on. "Couldn't you choose something else? We have three full aisles about the Industrial Revolution."

"Or moon-landing conspiracy theories," the other one interjected.

"Sounds exciting, but not today," William said firmly.

"Okay!" cried the black ladder, zooming off so quickly its wheels squealed.

"We'll meet back here once we've found what we need," William called to Iscia before the ladders each turned in different directions and shot into the stacks.

"All right," Iscia called back, sounding less than thrilled.

William's stepladder was moving extremely fast. He climbed up a couple more rungs so he could see where they were going. He had to hold on tightly with both hands. The stepladder turned right and then left and then continued straight ahead at an insane speed. Suddenly it screeched to a halt.

"Tobias Wenton," the stepladder announced in a monotone.

William looked around. They were in the very heart of the vast Archive. One of the overhead lights above him wasn't working, and it was a little darker here. A thick layer of dust covered the folders in front of him. This did not appear to be the most frequently visited part of the Archive.

"Is this whole shelf about Tobias Wenton?" William asked hopefully.

"No," the ladder replied curtly.

"Where is Tobias Wenton's folder?" William asked.

"Higher up," the ladder said, beginning to move upward.

William cast a quick glance down. They were already staggeringly high. He focused on the folders on the shelves, and suddenly the ladder stopped with a jerk. It stood there swaying alarmingly back and forth for a little bit before it stabilized.

"Professor Wenton," the ladder said.

William spotted a folder that had *T.W.* written by hand on its spine. He pulled it out and blew the dust off before opening it. His heart almost stopped at the sight of what was in it. Or to be more precise, what *wasn't* in it. Because apart from an old photograph, the folder was completely empty. William pulled out the picture and put the folder back where it belonged. He gasped when he realized what it was a picture of. Why in the world was—

A sound made him look up. He hurriedly shoved the picture into his pants pocket. He was not alone.

He heard sharp claws scraping against the floor.

"What's that?" William asked. He couldn't see anything from the top of the stepladder.

"What's what?" the vertical bot asked.

"That sound. It sounded like . . . an animal?"

"Probably Laika," the ladder said.

"Laika . . . ," William repeated. He remembered the sign hanging by the entrance. "Who's Laika?"

The ladder didn't respond. Something scratched past on the other side of the shelf. "Is Laika dangerous?" William asked.

"Only when you get too close," the ladder said.

"I have what I need," William said, looking around. "Find Iscia and get us out of here."

Then the lights went out. William stood there listening.

In the pitch black, the only sound was his own heart, which was beating like a galloping horse. Then he heard something moving below him again, sharp claws on the hard stone floor. Until that something stopped right beneath him.

William tried to remember how high he was. He cautiously leaned over the edge of the ladder and peeked down.

Then he saw it.

Two yellow eyes glowed at him from the darkness below. Then he heard a long, deep growl. William cautiously pulled back and stood there holding his breath.

"Please . . . please, go away, go away," he repeated quietly.

Then there was a clicking sound from the ceiling above him. *Click, click, click* . . . One light after another came on, and soon the whole Archive was bathed in light again. He glanced down. The yellow eyes were gone.

"Get me out of here!" William cried.

"Are you sure you don't want to take a peek at the Industrial Revolution?" the ladder tried.

"Totally sure," William said.

The rungs jerked, and the ladder lowered itself back down to the floor again. William looked around nervously. No sign of Laika, whatever Laika might be. Soon the ladder was zooming through the tall shelves at breakneck speed, back the way they had come.

They rounded a corner, and William saw Iscia standing on her stepladder about halfway up one of the shelves. She was staring at the folder she was holding open in front of her. It looked as if she'd found what she was looking for.

"Stop," William instructed the ladder.

The wheels screeched as the ladder skidded sideways and stopped next to Iscia.

"Did you find it?" William asked.

"Mm," she said, without looking at him.

"Is something wrong?" William asked. He thought she was acting a little strange, evasive even.

She closed the folder and tucked it under her jacket, still without looking at him. He decided that he would ask her later. They had more urgent matters to deal with.

"There's something in here called Laika. I think it's best we get out of here," he said, glancing behind him.

"Laika?" she asked, and finally met his eyes.

"Yeah, with glowing eyes," William said. "Let's go."

He was about to tell the vertical bot to step on it but stopped when he suddenly spotted something in the corner of his eye. He turned his head and saw her: the old woman.

She was standing by a shelf a little distance away, just standing there, completely still, staring at him with cold eyes. The little hummingbird was still sitting on her shoulder.

"Iscia," he whispered, without taking his eyes off the old woman. Iscia turned around.

"What do we do now?" she whispered back.

"I'll count to three—then I'll pull you over onto my ladder. Your stepladder will block the aisle so she won't be able to follow us," William whispered as he leaned out and took hold of Iscia's arm. "One . . . two . . . three!"

Iscia jumped.

"Go!" William cried out. The old lady started walking toward them.

"Where to?" the ladder asked.

"Anywhere, as long as it's out of here," William yelled back. "Quick!"

"Out it is, then," the ladder said as it backed up, turned abruptly, and zoomed off.

William peeked back at the old woman, who had started running, faster and faster. "She's having trouble with your ladder now," William cried, glancing at Iscia's ladder, which was blocking the space between the shelves.

He gasped as the old woman jumped over the tall ladder and kept coming toward them.

"Okay. This isn't going to go well," he muttered to himself.

Suddenly William saw the old woman split in half in the middle. The top half of her body separated just above her hips, dove forward, and landed on her hands. Her legs and hips picked up the pace.

"What?" William gasped as he stared at the two halves that were following them.

Then the two parts morphed into two men. William recognized them immediately.

They were the chauffeurs.

"You two have been on a little outing, I see." Goffman was standing next to the big globe in his office. William glanced over at Iscia, who was still holding her folder in her hands.

"We were just . . . ," William began, but stopped. They'd been caught red-handed. There was no point trying to explain it away.

Goffman pointed at Iscia. "She stays," he told the man who was holding her. "Get William back to his room. I'll deal with him later."

William tried to make eye contact with Iscia, but she avoided his gaze. Why was she acting so strange? Had she seen something in her folder?

★　★　★

"Welcome back . . . You got caught, I understand?" the door said, shutting.

William proceeded into the room without answering.

"You think it was me, don't you? I can assure you that I had nothing to do with it," the door said apologetically.

"You were the only one who knew I went out," William said, annoyed.

"Don't be naive," the door said. "The Institute has eyes and ears everywhere. I actually don't understand how you managed to get as far as you did before you were caught. What were you looking for?"

William pulled the photo out of his pocket. "It doesn't matter. The folder was almost empty. And then those two guys who brought me here showed up. First they were an old woman; then they split in two. I don't think they're human."

"Hybrids," the door said.

"Hybrids?" William repeated. "As in a little human and a little machine . . . like the plants in the garden?"

"Something like that," the door said. "There are some of them here at the Institute. So advanced that it's impossible to see the difference between them and regular people."

William was surprised. "Like who?" he asked.

"No idea. It's strictly secret. Only a few—" The door stopped as an alarm started wailing somewhere in the Institute. "Strange," the door muttered to itself.

"What's going on?" William asked.

"Don't know. Nobody mentioned a fire drill, either. Must be something important though," the door said.

William sat down on the bed and looked at the photo. He recognized the subject. It was a picture of the old desk he'd inherited from his grandfather. Someone must have emptied out his grandfather's folder. But had they forgotten to take the picture? Or was this a message . . . from his grandfather?

Suddenly the door opened, and one of the chauffeurs marched in. He came right over to William, picked him up, and slung him over his shoulder.

The gate to the cybernetic garden opened and the red-headed man proceeded inside with William flung over his shoulder. The alarm wailed in the distance.

The plants reached for them and hissed. The man hissed back, and the plants retreated in fear. Where were they going? Was he about to become plant food?

They made their way straight for the little oasis in the middle of the conservatory. Once inside, the man set William down and went to stand beside the other chauffeur.

Fritz Goffman took a step forward. Next to him William saw one of the strangest things he had ever seen. Its body was made of mirrorlike metallic parts with a completely normal dog head.

William recognized those glowing yellow eyes right away. This couldn't be anything other than the thing that had been trying to get him in the Archive.

Goffman patted the big doglike thing on the head. "I understand you've met Laika before."

William nodded.

Another alarm started wailing not far from where they were. "Why are the alarms going off?" William asked.

Goffman didn't respond. He looked up at the big clock that sat in the hands of the statue in the fountain. It seemed as if he were waiting for something. It was only now that William detected the presence of something he hadn't expected to see in Goffman's eyes.

Fear.

Something was very wrong.

He jumped when the door suddenly opened and Professor Slapperton stumbled in, out of breath.

"It's i–i–inside the Institute," he stuttered.

"It knows he's here," Goffman said, glancing at William.

"Who knows?" William asked, his voice trembling.

And then William heard something he'd heard before. Something he would never forget.

Branches snapping and heavy steps that thundered through the garden. The steps were getting closer. The thing coming toward them was the same thing that had attacked his house back in Norway.

"Come on!" Goffman yelled, waving to William. Slapperton got ready and jumped up into the fountain. The fish swam to the side, and a couple of them stuck their heads up out of the water and spit at him. But Slapperton wasn't very concerned about spitting fish right now. He grabbed the statue's arm and pulled down with all his might. A loud scream was heard, and something came racing toward them through the air. One of the man-eating plants crashed to the ground right next to William and lay there writhing.

"Come on!" yelled Goffman again, stepping into the fountain. Laika whimpered and jumped in behind him.

The two redheaded men did the same. One of them stopped beside William, eyeing Goffman with a look that said *Do you want me to drag him?*

William hurriedly climbed into the fountain.

He'd had enough of being thrown around for one day.

28

They moved quickly downward. A solid iron hatch closed
above them. The little group stood there in silence while the
fountain-elevator continued deeper and deeper down into
the darkness. William wondered how far down they were
going. He glanced at the others. The silence was unbearable.
He just had to break it.

"What about Iscia?" William looked up at Goffman.

"What about her?" Goffman asked in return.

"Is she in danger?"

"She's safe with the others."

The fountain jerked. It stopped, and the wall in front of
them opened. "Come on!" Goffman said.

Laika bounded after him. Slapperton gestured for
William to get out. And soon they were hurrying down a

long hallway without any doors or windows. William's ears needed to pop. He tried swallowing, but that didn't help.

After a while they stopped in front of a massive door that looked like the kind you would find in a bomb shelter. Slapperton held his thumb in front of a sensor on the wall, and the door slid open.

"Welcome, Professor Slapperton," said a voice that William thought he recognized.

"Thanks, Malin," Slapperton said, proceeding into the room.

"Welcome to the Institute's Ultra-Secret Department," Slapperton whispered. "This way."

William looked around.

They were surrounded by machines of every conceivable size and shape. Some of them were labeled: DEGENERATOR, SHRINKOMAT, TIME SQUEEZER, ANTIMATTER DEVELOPER. He followed Slapperton past a rusty barrel that said PAST TURBINE and stopped.

A new door came into view ahead of them that said TO THE VACUUM TRAIN on it. Slapperton raised his thumb to the fingerprint sensor on the wall.

No reaction.

"Just my luck," he said with growing panic in his voice, and tried again.

"Is something wrong?" Goffman asked.

Slapperton tried his other thumb, still no reaction.

"It's not working," he said. "Someone must have—"

Then the lights went out.

They stood there in the utter darkness. There was a thundering blast above them. "It's in," Slapperton whispered. "This way," he continued, pointing a small flashlight into the darkness.

He pulled open a red fire door. William and the others were right behind him. Slapperton shined the light downward into the darkness, revealing a narrow stairway. A new boom shook the stairs. Goffman's long legs took the stairs three at a time. William had trouble keeping up. He had to run to keep the same speed as Goffman.

When they reached the bottom, the whole thing exploded above them. William looked up and saw flames and smoke surging down toward them.

"Hurry!" Slapperton yelled, pointing to a train car ahead of them.

William looked around. It seemed like they had reached some kind of subterranean platform.

"Get in!" Slapperton yelled.

On the inside it was like a regular train. There were two rows of seats, one on each side. But the seats looked more like the ones you'd find in a racecar, with deep headrests and harness-style seat belts.

"Buckle up!" Slapperton yelled, sitting down in the front. The walls of the train were booming.

"It's right outside!" Goffman cried.

Slapperton pushed two red buttons at the same time and leaned back.

"Let's hope this works," he said, closing his eyes. "Hold on tight and lean your head back against the headrest."

A new boom hit the wall right by William. Then they heard a deep rumble followed by a loud whoosh, and they were pressed back into their seats. The acceleration was so violent that William couldn't move.

After a while the pressure let up and everything normalized again. William sat up and looked around.

"Are we moving?" he asked.

"You bet," said Slapperton. A proud smile lurked in the corner of his mouth. "We're already up around five hundred miles per hour. It will stabilize at a little over one thousand."

"One thousand?" William blurted out. He tried to imagine how fast that actually was.

"Yup," said Slapperton. "We're moving at speeds faster than an airliner. And the speed of sound. If we weren't moving in a perfect vacuum, we would break the sound barrier when we pass seven hundred sixty miles per hour."

"Wow," William said.

Then a scary thought hit him.

"What if we crash?" he said.

"Let's not think about that," said Slapperton.

Slapperton unbuckled his seat belt and stretched his legs.
Laika did a couple of rounds of the train car and then lay
down at Goffman's feet. The big dog closed its glowing eyes
and started purring like a cat. William glanced over at the
two chauffeurs, who were sitting a little way away.

He turned to Slapperton. "What was that thing that
attacked us up there?"

"A kind of machine," Slapperton replied.

"The same one that attacked my family back home in
Norway?" William asked.

"Probably," Slapperton said.

"A robot?"

"Yes, I suppose you could call it that. Very advanced," Slapperton said. "Once you realize it's there, it's generally too late."

"Is it . . . Abraham Talley's robot?" William asked.

Slapperton and Goffman looked at each other. "We think so," Slapperton said.

"Where are we going?" William continued.

"London," Slapperton said. "To the safest place we can stay right now. The Center for Misinformation."

"Misinformation?" William said.

"Yes, the Center for Misinformation is run by Professor Wellcrow. She was another one of the Institute's original founders."

"I thought my grandfather founded the Institute?" William said.

"There were three of us who founded the Institute. Your grandfather, Professor Wellcrow, and Fritz Goffman." Slapperton leaned forward, put his elbows on his knees, and looked long and seriously at William. "I think it's time you knew what was going on," he finally said. William nodded expectantly. He agreed completely.

"Do you remember what I showed you in the cellar below the Institute?"

"Yes," William hesitated. He did not like the idea that his grandfather had stolen something.

"The luridium that went missing?" Slapperton continued.

"Yes, I remember all that," William said, a little disconcerted.

"Well, as I told you, luridium is an intelligent metal.

We don't know who made it or why. But it's very old," Slapperton continued. "It can think for itself, but needs to be in contact with a living organism in order to work. That's why luridium can lie dormant for very long periods of time. Right up until someone finds it. I'm sure you also remember that Abraham Talley was the first person in the modern era to find a clump of luridium?"

William nodded.

"When Abraham found the luridium, it entered his body and he fell into a coma. He was taken to a hospital, but disappeared a couple of days later. You recall what happened to the other miners?"

"Yes," said William. He was beginning to feel impatient. They'd been through this all before. He wanted to know what had happened to his grandfather.

"When the area where the miners died was examined, the investigators discovered an ancient, impenetrable iron door covered with inscriptions," Slapperton continued. "The construction work was halted, and they spent a long time trying to decipher the writing. But only a few of the symbols could be understood: 'chamber' and 'technology.'"

Slapperton glanced at Goffman and gestured for him to proceed. Goffman cleared his throat solemnly.

"Not far from the iron door, they found a mechanical sphere . . . an orb. It was also covered with unintelligible symbols. But none of the symbols matched the ones on the iron door. They couldn't see any connection. After several years they gave up trying to decipher the symbols. In sheer desperation to get in, they detonated a tremendous explosion, which caused large sections of the tunnel system to collapse. Many lives were lost. After that the project was terminated, without results. The tunnel where the iron door is located was sealed up, and work on the train system continued in the other tunnels."

"What happened to the orb?" William asked.

"The orb was hidden away in a vault in the cellar of a museum in Oxford," Goffman said. "No one understood what it was or what it could be used for. As the years passed, both the orb and the sealed-up tunnel were forgotten."

"What happened to Abraham?" William asked.

"No one knows. He didn't turn up again until a hundred years later, at the beginning of the 1960s. He broke into the museum and tried to get the orb. But he was discovered, and then he disappeared again without getting what he'd come for.

"Your grandfather, Professor Wellcrow, and I were students at Oxford then. We realized there was something special about this strange metal sphere that nobody knew what it was. It didn't have a name, so we just called it an orb.

"We started digging into the history of the orb, which led us to the history of the forgotten iron door beneath London. We even got hold of some old notes on the symbols on the door. Your grandfather managed to decipher many of them, and that's how we first heard about luridium. We realized that there might be more luridium behind the iron door, and that the orb was actually a kind of key. When we realized how things fit together, that the luridium had entered Abraham's body, and how dangerous luridium could be, we established the Institute. We wanted to protect people by containing and concealing the luridium. We kept looking for the iron door. But we also started searching the world, hunting for other underground passageways, for more luridium. The small amount we found, we hid away at the Institute. We couldn't take the chance that it would end up in the wrong hands."

"What about the iron door?" William asked. "Did you find it?"

"All traces of it disappeared when London was bombed during the Second World War. And the underground system is sprawling," Slapperton said. "But your grandfather was responsible for the orb key. And he was obsessed with the idea of finding the iron door. Shortly before he disappeared he told me he had made a big breakthrough. Then you and your father were in that accident. Of course he dropped everything he was working on and went to take care of you. And when he disappeared right after that, we lost our best chance of getting into the chamber behind the iron door."

"So you started to look for other people who could get you through the door?" William said.

"Yes," said Goffman. "We arranged code-breaking contests all over the world. And we started collecting candidates that way. The orbs at the Institute are copies of that original orb. But we also knew that you had probably inherited your grandfather's talent for codes. And we devoted a lot of resources to locating you. Who'd have guessed you were hiding in Norway?"

"Do you think my grandfather was able to open the door, and that he's in there . . . somewhere?" William asked.

"That's what we're hoping," said Slapperton, and then he leaned farther forward as if he were going to divulge some terrible secret. "Personally I think he opened the door a long time before he disappeared. For some reason or other he just didn't tell us."

"And you want me to try to open the door?" William peered at them both.

"First we have to find it. I think you can get your orb to show us the way," Goffman said. "It's important that we find your grandfather, but also that we gain control over whatever's in there so that Abraham doesn't get hold of it. If we're right that there's luridium in there, it would be a catastrophe if Abraham got to it first," Goffman said.

"But could my grandfather have survived for so long in there?" William said.

"That I don't know," Slapperton said. "We can only hope. Your grandfather is a smart man."

"Slowing down," Malin announced over the loudspeaker. "We will be arriving at the Center for Misinformation in three minutes."

30

Slapperton stood beside a tall counter waiting for the woman seated behind it to finish on the phone. William and Goffman stood right behind him. Laika was wandering around, eyes darting about nervously. She clearly didn't like this place. They were in a big room with enormous glass walls and a revolving door leading out to the street. There was a fountain towering in the middle of the room. William thought it looked like the fountain at the Institute.

The woman behind the counter finished her phone call. She set down the phone and looked up at Slapperton with a fake smile.

"Yes . . . ?" she said.

"We're here to see Professor Wellcrow," Slapperton said.

"Sorry, but there's no one by that name working here," the woman said, still smiling.

Slapperton rolled his eyes in annoyance.

"Come on. Do we have to go through this charade every time I come here?"

"I've never seen you before," the woman said politely.

An irritated Slapperton shoved his hand into his jacket and pulled out a black wallet with pictures of small planets on it. He opened it and pulled out a card, which he handed to the woman. She took it, studied it for a moment, handed it back, and then picked up her phone.

"Have a seat. She'll be right with you."

"Welcome, welcome," a loud female voice called out.

William looked up and saw a little golf cart zooming toward them. But the cart didn't have any wheels. It glided above the smooth floor on a big, black hovercraft base.

"Professor Wellcrow," called Slapperton.

The woman behind the wheel smiled. She was wearing a gray, striped dress and had short black hair. She wore a pair of dark sunglasses.

The golf cart did a lap around the big fountain in the middle of the hall and came to an abrupt stop right in front of them.

"Jealous?" Professor Wellcrow crowed, leering at Slapperton. "I just got it last week."

"Hovercraft technology?" Slapperton asked.

"Anti-isotope hovercraft. Beta version," she said, smiling proudly.

"Of course." Slapperton nodded.

William was staring at the professor's sunglasses. A pair of thin wires ran from her glasses into the professor's forehead.

William leaned over to Goffman and whispered so she wouldn't hear. "What kind of glasses are those?"

"She's blind, but they allow her to see," Goffman whispered back.

"Could we go someplace where we can speak in private?" Slapperton said.

The professor's expression became serious. "Hi there. Well, I see this isn't just a friendly visit," she whispered before turning around 180 degrees. "Climb on, gentlemen."

After a breakneck trip, the hovercart stopped at a door that said ANTIAUDIO CHAMBER.

"After you," Professor Wellcrow said as the door opened and they walked in. The chauffeurs and Laika remained outside.

The room was empty. The walls were upholstered with something that resembled sofa cushions. Wellcrow put her index finger over her lips to indicate that they shouldn't say anything yet. She walked over to a control panel on the wall and pushed a couple of buttons. A quiet rushing sound poured out of little speakers mounted up under the ceiling.

"Intelligent sound cancellation," she said, nodding up at the speakers. "Now it's safe to talk."

She surveyed her three visitors, her eyes coming to rest on William.

"Is that him?" she asked.

"Yes," said Slapperton.

"We've met before. Did you know that?" she said.

"No," William replied, shaking his head.

"You were just a little baby, a newborn. Of course I had my eyes back then. You were a cute little thing." She paused. Then she turned to Slapperton. "What's going on?"

"It found us," Slapperton whispered.

"I figured it must be something like that," she said seriously. "I mean, we've known this day would come. Are you going to try to find the iron door?"

"Yes," Slapperton said. "We need somewhere to stay until tomorrow."

Professor Wellcrow keyed in a code, and the door to the Antiaudio Chamber opened again with a whoosh. "We have to get you to safety," she said, waving William out of the room.

The hovercart zoomed down the long hallway at a ridiculous speed. Professor Wellcrow pulled a phone out of her pocket and dialed a number.

"It's me. We're on our way down to the cellar. It's a code eleven. Yes, code eleven. No, this is not a drill," she said.

An alarm went off almost immediately.

Then booms could be heard as heavy doors slammed shut throughout the big building. The lights in the hallway flickered a little, before dimming and becoming stable.

"We switched over to our internal power supply," Wellcrow said. "We're officially cut off from the world."

"We haven't needed to use these cells for a long time, but they're updated periodically," Professor Wellcrow explained as they came down into the cellar. "You'll each get a room. They were built to keep things out, but it's easy for *you* to get out if anything should happen. There's an emergency hatch in each room that will take you right out of the building. I don't think that I need to add that the hatches should only be used in an emergency," she continued.

"Of course," Slapperton said, casting a nervous glance at Goffman.

31

William lay on the bed in the little cell. His eyes rested on a red hatch in the wall next to the bed. EMERGENCY EXIT it said in large, black letters. His mind was racing with all the information he'd learned on the train. It was as if his head were on fire. He held his orb in both hands on his chest. For some reason or other he felt safer when he held it that way.

Could he trust what Slapperton and Goffman had told him? Just thinking about it made his head spin.

The mattress was hard, but he felt sleep creeping over him all the same. His thoughts turned to fog, and keeping his eyes open became a struggle until finally he let them close.

"William," a voice whispered.

William sat up in bed. He'd been sound asleep. He rubbed

his eyes and squinted around the room. The silhouette of a man was standing in the middle of the room. The figure was flickering slightly. Suddenly it disappeared and then appeared again. *A hologram!* William thought.

"William . . . ," the voice repeated.

William stared, not quite sure. Could it really be . . . "Grandpa?" he whispered.

The hologram didn't respond. William realized that it was probably a recording. He got up and cautiously walked a couple of paces closer. He recognized the old man in front of him from pictures. It really was his grandfather.

"William, I don't know how old you'll be when you see this, and I don't know how much you already know. But since you've come here, I'm assuming you've already found out some. Let me start with the most obvious. My name is Tobias Wenton. I'm your grandfather." He paused briefly. "You've grown up surrounded by secrets. And I'm sure you've wondered what's going on. It is only fair that you should know everything. Especially since soon I'm going to ask you to do something important for me."

His grandfather paused before continuing.

"When you were three and a half years old, you and your father were in a serious traffic accident. Your spine was damaged, crushed, I suppose is the right word. I was at a dig in Tibet when it happened. I dropped everything and caught the first flight home to London. Your father was in a coma with a broken neck and you . . . there wasn't anything the doctors could do, just give you morphine and wait while nature took its course. I had to do something. I had no choice. There was only one thing that could save you."

Grandfather paused again before he continued.

"I knew the Institute would never let me have it. They would never let it be removed from the vault. Not even for me, or my grandson. So I was left with only one option . . . I had to steal it. After I gave you the luridium, you got better. But the Institute came after me. Abraham Talley, too. I was under attack from all sides. I had stolen the only luridium we'd managed to find. I had to get away. Draw the attention away from you."

Grandfather adjusted his glasses.

"I knew that by giving you the luridium I would be creating what the Institute and I had been working so hard to prevent: luridium spreading to people and finally . . ."

Grandfather paused again.

"When a person gets luridium into their system, the luridium takes over the injured parts of the body. In your case this was the spine and parts of your brain. Even before the accident I could tell that you had a special knack for code breaking. Once you had the luridium in you, I knew this talent would be multiplied a hundredfold. That makes you the very best cryptographer in the world, William. So you have to be careful. There are a lot of people who want to use you. Without the luridium you wouldn't have survived, but you're not quite as human as you thought you were . . . you're forty-nine percent luridium, William."

Everything went black before William's eyes. His legs felt like jelly, and he fell to his knees. He couldn't believe it. Did he have luridium inside him? He looked at his hands. Besides shaking in shock, they seemed totally normal. His head was exploding with questions. He looked up at Grandfather.

"I know it's a lot to process, William," Grandfather continued. "You have to give it time, and let it sink in."

"But how?" William stuttered. He was still dazed from the shock. "How can I be full of luridium . . . I still feel like . . . myself."

William knew he was talking to a hologram and that he wouldn't get a reply. But he asked anyway. He just had to say it out loud, for his own sake.

Grandfather's hologram didn't say anything more for a while. It was like he wanted to give William some time to react. Think things over.

Then Grandfather smiled and continued. "I bet you're bursting with questions that you want to ask me. But that will have to wait. There are more urgent matters at hand."

William knew that Grandfather was right. There was no use asking questions now. He had to concentrate. He felt that there was more important information coming.

"You're different from everyone else," the hologram continued. "You have a special talent. The codes."

Grandfather paused again. Like he needed a break. He removed his glasses and cleaned them with his shirt. Then he put them back on.

"Abraham wants to get his hands on what's inside you. And if he finds you . . ." His grandfather stopped. As if just the thought of what would happen was totally paralyzing to him.

"The most important thing for you now is to find me. My body is cryogenically frozen in a secret bunker in the tunnels deep beneath Victoria Station," continued the hologram, which blinked a bit like it was losing power. William moved closer.

"It's important that you come alone. I don't think you can trust the others. Use your powers to find me. You have to let go of yourself and let the luridium inside you be your guide. And bring your orb. You won't be able to get in without it."

The hologram hissed and blinked again.

"Find the cryogenic chamber behind the large metal gates. You'll need to decipher them to get in. But I think that you're the only one, besides me, who can do it. There are ten cryogenic tanks down there. It's very important that you only thaw number seven." His grandfather took a small pause and looked very serious. "Number seven," he repeated to make sure it had really sunk in.

The lights in the room blinked. The hologram of his grandfather quivered a couple of times and then disappeared with a zap.

"Grandpa?" William said, but there was no response.

William stood there in the middle of the room. Was this really true? Was he 49 percent intelligent metal? In other words, a kind of machine?

He touched his face with a trembling hand. He felt the same as before, human. He needed air.

He had to get out. His eyes turned to the red emergency hatch in the wall.

32

William hit the snow face-first. He lay there gasping for breath. He didn't know how long he'd been running or how far he'd come. After he'd made it out of the Center for Misinformation, he'd hardly looked back. The emergency hatch had shot him out onto a dark backstreet. From there he had just run.

It had been snowing hard for the last hour, and there wasn't much warmth in his thin tweed jacket. His only company up until this point had been snowplows and taxis, but by now the streets were full of people.

When he caught his breath, he sat up. He was in a big park. Busy people scurried by.

Suddenly he heard someone behind him say, "William."

He recognized the voice and turned around right away.

"Iscia?" he whispered.

Iscia helped him up and pulled him along. "Come on," she whispered.

A little while later William and Iscia were sitting in a small café. Pleasant piano music streamed out of a small speaker in the ceiling. The café was half-full of people standing in line to buy their morning coffee. William and Iscia were sitting in a quiet corner right by the window. Iscia kept glancing out the window, as if she was waiting for someone. Or was scared.

William rubbed his hands against his thighs and felt like he was starting to get the feeling back in his fingers. A smiling woman came over to them.

"What can I get for you?" she asked.

"Uh." William cleared his throated. "I don't have any . . ."

"I have money," Iscia said, looking up at the waitress. "Could we have two large pancakes with whipped cream and two cups of hot chocolate? Also with whipped cream?"

The woman jotted their order down on her notepad and left.

They sat there in silence for a bit. William looked around. Everything seemed so normal.

"What are you doing here?" he asked.

"I ran away," she said, a little worried.

"Why?"

"I'd rather not talk about it."

"How did you find me?" he asked.

"It wasn't that hard, actually," Iscia said. "Taking the vacuum train to the Center for Misinformation when the Institute is under attack is standard procedure."

William hesitated. It just seemed too simple. She had found him too easily. Could he really trust her? He needed to know more.

"Is the Institute attacked often?" William asked.

"No," she said. "At least never while I've been there."

"So how do you know about the vacuum train?" said William.

"I've read the rules," she said, smiling slyly. "Don't you trust me?"

William didn't answer, just stared at her. He could see her squirming a bit now. Like she was looking for something to say.

"When you, Goffman, and Slapperton all suddenly disappeared after the attack," she continued, "I figured you'd escaped by vacuum train. I was tired of the Institute and all the machines anyway. I needed a bit of a change."

William decided to let his suspicions rest for a while. He was glad she was here.

"How's everyone else? Was anyone injured?" William asked.

"Whatever attacked disappeared right afterward," she

said. "It seems like it was only interested in you guys. Do you have any idea why?"

William shook his head and looked down at the café table.

"Are you all right?" she asked, her voice worried.

"Yeah," William said, without looking up.

He was dying to tell her everything, that he was part metal like a machine. He needed to share it with someone, but he couldn't. His grandfather had told him not to tell anyone. Besides, he wasn't sure how Iscia would respond.

He looked up at her. She smiled back at him. He suddenly thought about her strange reaction when she had found her folder. That was the last time he had seen her, up until today. He had to ask her about it.

"Can I ask you something?" he said.

"What?" she said.

"You remember back at the Institute . . . when you found your folder," he said.

She stopped smiling. Like she was suddenly reminded of something bad.

"Why did you react like that?" he continued.

She looked down, scraping at a small crack in the table with a fingernail.

"I'd rather not talk about it," she whispered. "Do you mind?"

"Okay," he said. "But—"

He was interrupted by the server returning with steaming-hot pancakes and two big cups of hot chocolate. She smiled at them.

"Enjoy!" she said, and left.

William was glad the food was here. He was starving, and the conversation had gotten much too serious. He took a bite and closed his eyes. For a brief second he dreamed he was far away. It was like being home again. His mother always made pancakes for breakfast on Sundays. He took a big gulp of the cocoa and felt the warmth spread through his body. He opened his eyes, glanced at Iscia, and smiled. She smiled back.

"Why are you alone? Where are the others?" she asked, taking a big bite of her pancake.

William hesitated.

He didn't really know what to say. Could he trust her? He hadn't forgotten that Goffman had wanted to talk to her after she'd found the folder. He sat there, mulling this over for a bit. But if he couldn't trust her, who could he trust? He decided to tell her a little.

"I ran away. Just like you," he said, smiling apologetically.

"You ran away? Why?" she asked. "Does this have something to do with your grandfather? Did you find anything in his folder in the Archive?"

"Yeah, it has something to do with him," William said, hesitating. "Someone is after me."

"Who?"

"I can't say very much, Iscia. Maybe I can tell you more later. After things have calmed down."

"But then what's your plan? Are you going to run around London alone?" she asked.

"I have to find my grandfather. He's . . . ," William began, but stopped when he glanced out the window and spotted an old woman standing on the sidewalk. He recognized her right away. It was the old woman from the Institute. Or, as he now knew, it was the two chauffeurs.

"We have to go," he said, pulling Iscia with him. "They found us."

After running for what felt like forever, William and Iscia finally stopped outside the main entrance to Victoria Station. William wiped the sweat off his face and looked around.

"There she is," Iscia whispered, pointing to something across the street.

And sure enough, the old woman was pushing her way through the crowd on the sidewalk. Her eyes were trained on William. She walked right out into the street. A bus had to slam on its brakes to avoid hitting her, but she kept going as if nothing had happened.

"Come on," William said, pulling Iscia along.

They ran down the steps into Victoria Underground Station and were swallowed up by the enormous throng of people in the concourse. They stopped in front of a long row of automatic ticket barriers.

"How do we get through these?" William asked, looking nervously behind him.

"Watch this," Iscia said, and hurried after an overweight man who pressed his Oyster car against the electronic reader. She followed him through the ticket barrier.

"Look!" she called, pointing to the old woman, who was coming down the stairs behind William.

He got a running start and then jumped over one of the gates that was meant for wheelchair users and baby carriages. A deep male voice rang out behind him, "Hey you!"

William turned around and saw that a station guard had seen him.

"Run, William!" Iscia cried.

She turned and ran toward the escalators that led underground. William set out after her.

The escalators were full of people and were creeping downward at a snail's pace. William looked back. The guard was gone, but the old woman was right behind him. She was pushing people out of her way with her cane and getting dangerously close.

"This way," William said, climbing up onto the raised central area in between the two escalators. He sat down on his rear end and slid down.

Iscia did the same. They slid fast.

A little too fast.

William crashed into a man who was standing at the end of the escalators playing his violin. They both fell to the ground. The violin slid across the floor.

"Sorry, sorry," mumbled William as he dragged himself to his feet. The violinist stood up, dazed, and looked around for his violin.

"Watch out!" cried Iscia as she careened into them before landing with both feet on the floor.

William hurriedly picked up the violin and helped the violinist to his feet again. "Sorry," he shouted before he and Iscia vanished into the crowd on the platform.

"Get down," William called to Iscia.

Soon they were crawling on all fours across the filthy platform. William stopped. "Listen," he said.

It was the sound of a train approaching. They got up and walked hunched over toward the far end of the platform.

Suddenly William spotted something—something small and shiny—moving. He stopped and looked around, but it was gone. Was he starting to see things? He kept going but stopped when he saw it again. Something darted between the legs of the people ahead of him and then was gone.

"What is it?" asked Iscia, who was right behind him.

"I thought I saw something . . ." He spotted the little beetle peeking out from behind a briefcase sitting on the floor a little way away. "The beetle?" William blurted out.

The little beetle darted toward them in a zigzag.

"What is that?" Iscia whispered.

"That's the little beetle that came to my room right before my family was attacked back home," William said.

"*Attacked* back home?" Iscia repeated.

William watched as the beetle hopped up and down before turning around and darting away toward the edge of the platform.

"It got me out of the house," he said. "Maybe it's trying to help us now?"

The train thundered into the station, the doors opened, and people poured out. The beetle darted onto the train and vanished in between all the feet.

"We have to get on," William said.

William and Iscia pushed their way into the end car. William cast a glance back and spotted the old woman pushing her way into the same car. The doors closed behind her, and the train started moving again.

William squatted down next to Iscia.

"She got on. She's in here," he whispered.

"What do we do now?" Iscia whispered back.

The little beetle was in front of them, bouncing around as if awaiting instructions. William cautiously stood up. The old woman was still standing over by the doors.

Her narrow eyes slowly scanned the crowd. William ducked down again.

"We have to get out of here," he whispered. "She's by the doors. She'll find us when the train stops and people get off."

"How can we get off if she's blocking the doors?" Iscia whispered.

William thought that over. Then he had an idea. "Follow me. We don't have any choice. This is our only option."

William opened the door to the empty driver's compartment at the back of the car. They stopped at the door that led out the very back of the train. The little beetle fidgeted around eagerly next to them.

"Are you insane?" Iscia exclaimed. "Are we going to jump off a train traveling at full speed?"

"Do you have a better idea?"

William slid the door open, and they peered down at the tracks flashing by. There was a gap between the central electric rails. The beetle crawled up his pants leg and hid in the inside pocket of his tweed jacket.

"Come on," William said, waving to Iscia. "On the count of three," he said, taking her hand. "One . . . two . . . three!"

They jumped together, back and straight, so they landed in the space between the central rails. "Whoa," William exhaled, as he got to his feet and checked he was still in one piece. "That's what I call an emergency exit," he said, looking at Iscia.

"Well I don't think I got electrocuted," she said, testing her fingers for sparks.

"I think we got away," William said, pointing to the train, which was disappearing into the darkness.

"I really hope so," said Iscia. "What do we do now?"

"Let me think," said William, looking around.

Little lamps covered in soot were attached to the tunnel walls and gave off just enough light that they could more or less make out their surroundings. Something dripped from the ceiling, and the air smelled dank, musty, and old.

Suddenly Iscia grabbed William's upper arm. Her eyes were wide with fear. "Look," she whispered, her voice trembling, pointing into the tunnel where the train had gone.

William turned around and saw the old woman walking toward them.

"Come on. She hasn't seen us yet," William whispered, pulling Iscia along in the opposite direction.

William stopped and looked around at the tunnel. Except for a dirty light on the wall in front of them, everything was dark. They'd been running for a while and were dripping in sweat. Iscia stopped next to William and pointed at something on the ground in front of them. William jumped back as a fat rat darted across the tracks and vanished into a big crack in the wall.

"I hate rats," Iscia said dryly.

William was about to get going again when he heard a sound. It seemed like Iscia had heard it too.

"What is that rumbling?" she said.

A cool draft of air came out of the darkness toward them. The rumbling increased. William could feel the vibrations in the ground now.

"Train," he said quietly.

William looked around for somewhere to seek refuge.

"It's going to crush us," Iscia said, pointing at two glowing dots that were approaching menacingly.

The tunnel floor beneath them was really shaking. Panic rose in William, but he tried to hold it together.

"We have to get away from it!" Iscia pulled on his arm.

"Where?" William shouted over the roar of the oncoming train. He could see the front of it clearly now. It was only about thirty yards away.

"Up against the wall?" she shouted.

"There's not enough room." William pointed at the side of the train as he backed away. "It'll hit us."

"Run!" Iscia shouted, and waved at him.

They started running. But the mix of gravel and train tracks made it almost impossible. The train got closer with every step.

"Wave at the driver," Iscia shouted. "Maybe he'll manage to stop."

"Not enough time," William shouted back.

"Then we're about to be mincemeat," Iscia shouted. William could see the fear in her eyes now.

Then something occurred to him: the orb. He had it in his jacket pocket. It was a long shot. But the only shot he had. He got the orb out and turned it as he ran. Suddenly the display blinked to life and showed a number four. The level he had gotten to in the duel against Freddy.

"What are you doing?" shouted Iscia.

William threw the orb over his shoulder as he ran. He turned his head and looked at the orb as it bounced softly in midair. Then a wall of light, just like the one that had saved him from Freddy's orb, shot out. The train hit the wall, pushing the orb in front of it.

"It's slowing down," Iscia shouted.

William stopped and looked at the train slowing and eventually coming to a complete halt.

"You did it," Iscia shouted. "Get the orb. They're coming out." Iscia pointed up at the people inside the train. "If they catch us we're in big trouble."

William grabbed the orb, and the light wall disappeared. He turned just as a door slid open and a man in a uniform appeared in the opening.

"Hey!" the man shouted.

After a few minutes of running, William and Iscia came to a stop. William stood there panting like a wild animal. His lungs felt like they were going to explode.

"Now what?" Iscia asked.

"Well, we can't keep wandering around in these tunnels. There are only so many full-speed trains we can dodge," William said thoughtfully. "He said the orb would lead the way," he mumbled to himself.

"Who?" Iscia asked.

"My grandfather."

"You talked to him?" she asked.

"Yes. Well, in a way," William said, and then turned to face her. "It was a hologram. It just showed up last night." He hesitated. "My grandfather is down here somewhere, frozen. I have to thaw him out again."

"Frozen?" Iscia exclaimed.

"Yeah," William said, pulling his orb out of his chest pocket. Iscia stared into the dark tunnel.

"You don't have to come with me if you don't want to. It'll be dangerous," William said, looking at her.

"I don't have anything better do," she replied. "Besides, I don't really want to go back and run into that woman again. Or another train."

"I have to get this working," William said, closing his eyes and concentrating on his orb.

"You're going to do that now? Here?" he heard Iscia say.

He waited.

But nothing happened.

William clenched his teeth. He had to do this. He had to get to the next level. Had to trust his instincts.

"Come on," Iscia said. "I think I hear another train."

"You're not exactly helping," William said, irritated. "Let me concentrate."

And then he felt it.

It started in his stomach, like a faint ache below his belly button. The vibrations grew stronger and moved up his spine and out into his hands. His fingers started working. "Click . . . click . . . click . . . ," the orb said.

William opened his eyes and could see all the different symbols from the orb floating in front of him. Some were glowing brightly, others had faded to the background. He looked down at his hands. They moved quickly. Faster and faster. Now the only sound he could hear was the clicking from the orb.

Click . . . click . . . click . . . click.

Then his hands suddenly stopped, and the floating symbols descended down toward the orb and gently settled on the surface.

The orb floated up out of his hands. William opened his eyes. The orb hovered in the air in front of him. It twisted a bit from side to side as if it were orienting itself. Then a blue beam shot out of it and quickly moved from side to side over the walls and ceiling. Then the beam disappeared, and the orb started flying away down the tunnel. It didn't look like it was planning to wait for them.

"Come on," William said, following it.

After the orb led them through what felt like an interminable labyrinth of old, disused tunnels, it rounded a corner and paused.

William froze, staring ahead of him. Iscia stopped beside him.

"It tricked us," she cried.

There was nothing but a dirty brick wall in front of them.

"No! Look! It wants to keep going," William said.

The orb kept moving, slowly, straight ahead, stopping when it bumped into the wall.

Clack . . . clack . . . clack . . . The orb kept trying to get through the wall.

"I don't think it tricked us," William said, walking up to the brick wall.

He put his hand on the rough surface. "This is old," he said.

He thought about what Goffman had said about the sealed-up tunnel. "It's here. I just know it is." William took a couple of steps back.

If his grandfather had encountered this wall, he must have gotten past it somehow.

"Why right here? Why this one? We've already passed a ton of walls just like this," Iscia said. She walked over to the tunnel wall and ran her hand over the surface. "Do you really think there's a secret door here somewhere?"

William peered down at the ground below where the orb was hovering. He spotted something sticking up out of the gravel. It looked like a handle made of steel. He squatted down and started digging.

"Look here! I found something," he said. Iscia knelt down next to him and helped.

"It's some kind of lid," William said once he'd removed all the gravel. William ran his hand over something that looked like a manhole cover.

"Are we going to go down into the sewer?" Iscia said, wrinkling her nose.

"I don't think this is a sewer. It doesn't look that old. Maybe this is how my grandfather got in, by digging," William said, trying to lift the lid. But it wouldn't budge. "Help me!"

They both pulled with all their might, but it still wouldn't move. Suddenly William spotted something.

"What is it?" Iscia asked.

"Look at that!" he said, pointing to a line of symbols on the cover.

William recognized the symbols right away. He'd seen them before. Many times. He stuck his hand into his pocket and pulled out the old picture of his grandfather's desk.

"Of course," he said as he began brushing the sand away from around the steel frame surrounding the lid. A thin line came into view. "We don't lift it. We have to twist it. The whole lid is a kind of combination lock. Help me."

William studied the photograph of his grandfather's desk and looked at the order of the symbols that were carved into it. He hoped he was right. They didn't have any time to lose.

"To the left," William said, stuffing the photo back into his pocket and grabbing the handle.

Iscia grabbed the handle as well. They pulled. The lid turned surprisingly easily now. As if it was on ball bearings. When the first symbol hit the mark, the massive lock emitted a click from deep within.

Soon they had spun the lid back and forth through the whole set of symbols. The lid was getting increasingly harder to turn. There was only one turn left. William pulled on the lid. It was so hard to move now, and his hands were so exhausted, he thought he wouldn't make it.

"Look," Iscia cried, pointing into the darkness.

William looked up, and his heart practically stopped.

The old woman was running toward them from the dark. But she wasn't moving like an old woman anymore. She moved like a sprinter over the tracks. Her movements were lightning fast.

"Come on!" William cried through clenched teeth.

He pulled on the lid with all his might. Together he and Iscia managed to move it slightly. But not enough to reach the last symbol. William looked up at the old woman. She was about fifty yards away now, and running like a an Olympic sprinter. Without slowing down, she suddenly split in two as she ran, turning into the two chauffeurs.

William gathered all his last strength. He thought about his grandfather and how close he was to finally finding him, a burst of adrenaline shot through his veins, and he pulled like his life depended on it.

Suddenly there was a faint click from the lid . . . and it flipped up. A cloud of dust rose from the hole. A rusty metal ladder disappeared down into the darkness.

William grabbed hold of Iscia and pulled her toward the hole. "Get in!" he shouted.

Iscia jumped into the darkness. The beetle suddenly shot out from his jacket pocket and followed her down the hole.

William caught the hovering orb and cast a last glance at one of the chauffeurs, who lunged for him through the air like an attacking tiger.

He grabbed the lid and threw himself into the dark hole, pulling it shut after him.

"Iscia?" William whispered, listening.

He was surrounded by impenetrable darkness. All he could hear was the sound of the chauffeurs banging on the massive lid above him.

They wouldn't be able to solve the code anytime soon, William thought. But they probably had some kind of weapon or device to get through now that William had found the entrance. William knew they had to hurry before that happened.

"Iscia?" he whispered again. Nothing.

William fumbled ahead in the darkness. Gravel and sand crunched beneath his shoes as he walked. He found a stone wall with his hand and followed it until he came to a new wall right ahead of him. He couldn't go any farther, and he felt his panic rising. He had never liked confined spaces. He started breathing faster. The air down here was even worse than in the old tunnels.

"Where are you, Iscia?" he tried again, this time a little louder.

"Up here," he heard from somewhere higher up. "There's a ladder!"

William groped around until he found the rungs leading up. He started climbing.

Iscia was standing by a natural rock wall, running her hand over the surface of the stone. The little beetle rubbed itself affectionately against her leg.

"Isn't it beautiful?" she said, dreamily looking at the wall.

William stared at the faint blue light emanating from the rock face. He'd seen that light before, inside the container Slapperton had shown him in the cellar at the Institute. His whole body started trembling. It couldn't be far to that door and his grandfather now.

"Look at that," Iscia said, pointing to a wire hanging from the ceiling.

"Is that a light?" William walked closer. The blue gleam from the rock face gave off just enough light that he could barely make out their surroundings.

"Maybe there's a light switch in here too, then?" Iscia said.

William started looking around. In the distance he could hear pounding on the lid.

"I don't think we have much time," he said.

"Bingo," Iscia exclaimed.

There was a click as she flipped the switch, and a single light came on.

William shuddered.

They were standing in the middle of an unfinished tunnel. Old wooden beams lay around, and a few rusty pickaxes were leaning against the stone wall. The end of the tunnel had collapsed in a pile of rubble and boulders.

"It's here," William whispered.

"What is this?" Iscia asked.

She'd stopped by a big, dust-covered brass plate that was bolted to the side of the rock face. William walked over to her and wiped the dust off the plate. A chill ran down his spine as he read what it said: "In memory of those who perished."

"Did people die here?" Iscia whispered.

"Yes," William said.

"This is creepy," she said, pulling away.

But where was the door? William looked around. There was nothing here but an unfinished tunnel. He turned his attention back to the brass plate. Why was it so big when there was only one sentence on it?

William brought his hands up to the edge of the plate. He felt a cold draft of air. There had to be an opening behind it. He worked a couple of fingers in and pulled. The rusty screws that held the plate in place soon gave, and it fell to the ground with a clank.

In the wall behind there was a round metal hole. It looked like the end of some kind of concrete pipe and was just big enough for a grown man to crawl through.

Suddenly something moved inside the pipe. William pulled back as a black rat stuck its head out from the end and sniffed at them. Iscia picked up a small stone and threw it at the rat, which squeaked and backed into the darkness again.

"I really . . . really hate rats," Iscia said with disgust in her voice.

"Me too," said William. "But I think that's where we have to go. I can feel it." William put a hand on his stomach. He could feel a slight tremor, which usually meant he was close to some kind of code.

"I'll go first," Iscia said.

William looked at her. He could see that she wasn't kidding, but there was something in her eyes that told him that she really didn't want to go.

"I'll go," William said. "It's *my* grandfather we're looking for, remember. Besides . . . you *really* hate rats." William swallowed dryly, forced a smiled, and looked at the pipe.

"Okay," Iscia said. "I'll be right behind you."

William bent forward and reached into the dark pipe with his hands. It felt moist and slimy. He wanted to pull back, but the tremors had increased in strength, which meant that he was on the right track.

Soon William was on all fours, crawling through the pipe. In front of him he couldn't see anything but darkness. And the smell was almost unbearable. He had to use all of his concentration not to get overcome by claustrophobia. He could hear Iscia breathing behind him. It felt good to have her close.

William stopped as he suddenly spotted something in the dark: a round patch of light ahead.

"There it is," he whispered.

He started crawling again. Faster and faster.

He was so close. He had to get out.

William and Iscia stared. Neither said a word. The most beautiful thing William had ever seen stood before them. They were in a big cave. The rock walls around them pulsed in strong, blue light.

And a gigantic iron door towered in the middle of the cave wall. A pile of empty wooden crates sat beside the door. All with DYNAMITE written on the side. *Probably from the last attempt to blast through,* William thought.

The beetle moved restlessly between them. Tapping its little metal feet on the stone ground.

"What—what is that?" Iscia stammered.

"The door," William whispered.

He approached cautiously.

The door was covered with symbols. These were the

symbols his grandfather had managed to decipher. These were the symbols that told him about luridium and how dangerous it could be.

This was where Abraham Talley had found the first clump of the intelligent metal over 150 years ago. And maybe this was where his grandfather was now.

William held out his orb.

"Show me what to do," he whispered.

He closed his eyes and concentrated, trying to invoke the vibrations. But nothing happened.

"Come on, come on . . . ," he repeated.

"What are you waiting for?" he heard Iscia say.

"I'm trying," he said through clenched teeth. "I'm trying. . . ."

He stood there waiting, but nothing happened. He started to panic. Had he lost his gift, right when he needed it most?

William didn't know if it was because he was completely exhausted or because he'd found out he wasn't what he had always thought he was, but suddenly he felt completely powerless. How had he ever gotten himself into this situation? He had only himself to blame. Why couldn't he just have kept his fingers off the Impossible Puzzle that day in the museum? Then everything would have been like it was before. He should have listened to his parents. Then he would still be sitting in his room working on deciphering some harmless code or other. His father had been totally right: He should have stayed well away from codes. But now it was way too late. Nothing was like it used to be.

The only thing that kept him going now was the fact that he was closer to finding his grandfather than he had ever been. He had to go on. When he found Grandfather, everything would be okay again.

And then suddenly it was like he knew what he had to do. He had to accept what he was. There was no going back, he thought.

I am intelligent metal . . . I am intelligent metal, he repeated to himself. *I am two percent more human than metal.*

"They're coming through the wall . . . ," he heard Iscia say from somewhere far away.

But William couldn't respond. He couldn't even open his eyes. He felt that familiar ache in his belly. It grew and became much stronger than usual. Soon his whole spine was quivering. It felt like his body was going to shake apart. The vibrations spread to his arms and hands, and his fingers started working like crazy. The inside of the orb clicked and clicked.

Suddenly he opened his eyes, and he almost couldn't believe what he saw. The symbols on the big door were pulsating with a golden light. Some of the symbols rose up off the surface and hovered, coming toward him. They formed new patterns. He recognized many of them now.

Some he had seen on his grandfather's desk, while others were engraved in the orb. His fingers worked faster and faster. It was like he understood what the symbols meant now, as if he could suddenly read an ancient language. Even though he couldn't explain it, he suddenly understood what luridium was and how it could be used for good or evil. He understood why Abraham was so desperate for more, and he understood what kind of strength lay hidden deep within his own body. It was amazing and frightening at the same time.

The vibrations vanished, and his fingers stopped working. The orb floated up from his hands, glided over to the middle of the door, and then vanished into a hole.

"You did it!" he heard Iscia cheering behind him.

A rumbling came from deep inside the big door. William took a couple of steps back and watched as the door slowly slid open.

The next thing that happened was like a dream, hazy images and sounds that seemed very far away. Blue light. Iscia yelling and waving at him. William staggering after her into the darkness. Then the big door closing behind them with a deep *boom*.

"William? William! Can you hear me, William?"

Mostly he wanted to sleep. He was so unbelievably tired, needed to rest. It felt like that last puzzle had broken him.

"You have to wake up!" Iscia cried.

Slowly his hearing returned, and things seemed to come closer. His thoughts cleared.

"I'm—fine," he stammered, but he was still dizzy. "Where are we?"

"I don't know," Iscia said, standing up. "What kind of place is this?"

"Where are the chauffeurs?" William asked.

"They're on the other side of that," she said, pointing to the big iron door. "They were just about to get us when the door closed."

William got to his feet. His orb was hovering in the air next to him.

"It worked," he said to himself.

Then suddenly he thought of something. "Did you see what happened to the beetle?"

"Yeah. It went that way," Iscia said, pointing.

William turned around and gasped.

In front of them, an enormous hall stretched into the distance. Here and there, water drops fell from the carved-stone ceiling high above them. Rows of huge submarines towered in front of them.

"Wooow," William gasped.

His eyes traveled over the silent metal giants. Too many to count. Suddenly he felt insignificantly small.

Behind the submarines were rows of trucks, tanks, and military motorcycles that seemed to stretch endlessly into the gigantic hall.

"What is this? Some kind of military depot?" Iscia asked.

"Looks like it's from the Second World War," William

said, taking a couple of wobbly steps forward.

"Do you think anyone knows about this?" she asked.

"The Institute knows about it," William said. "And Abraham Talley, I'm betting. But I don't think any of them have managed to get in here. So why in the world is the ancient technology chamber full of equipment from the Second World War?"

William stood there for a bit, contemplating. Had Goffman and Slapperton been lying to him? Or did they not know about this?

"But why store submarines down here? There isn't even any water," Iscia said.

"I don't know," William said.

He stopped by one of the submarines and knocked on the metal with his fist.

"Do you think we're safe here?" Iscia asked, glancing at the gigantic door behind them.

"As long as we don't open it for them," William said, pointing to a lever on the wall next to the door. "It looks like it can only be opened from the inside. I just hope there's nothing in here we need to worry about. Come on."

They continued into the rows of military trucks.

"Is he in here somewhere, do you think? Your grand-father?" Iscia asked.

"That's what he said. We just have to find out where. We need to find container number seven."

They stopped in front of a red steel door. The sign on the red door said CRYOGENIC LAB.

"Frozen, right? It must be in here . . . ," Iscia said.

William put his hand on the handle. "It's locked."

He looked around and spotted a military tank parked a little way away. He started walking toward it.

"Um, have you ever driven something like that before?" Iscia asked.

"Has to be a first time for everything," he said matter-of-factly.

Inside the tank, Iscia sat down in the seat next to William and studied him as he ran his fingers over the instrument panel. His index finger stopped at one of the buttons.

"Sometimes you just have to trust your gut," he said, and pushed the button.

Iscia yelped as her seat back suddenly released and she found herself reclined all the way.

"Sorry," William said.

His finger kept moving and stopped at another button. He pushed it. The whole tank shook as its powerful motor started to rumble.

William pulled on both control levers and put his foot on the gas. The big tank jumped.

"Careful," Iscia said, taking a firm hold of her seat.

William twisted the stick to the side. The tank turned

around to aim its gun turret at the door. William pressed his thumb on a red button at the tip of one of the handles, and there was a sudden explosion that shook the entire tank.

Then it was quiet. William opened the hatch in the ceiling, and they both peeked out. "Wow." William's eyes widened.

Iscia smiled. The red metal door was gone. A dark, smoke-filled crater gaped back at them from where the door had been.

"There's no one here," William said.

Iscia followed him.

There were ten enormous containers in a row in front of them. The containers reached all the way to the ceiling, and were numbered from one to ten.

"Who could have made these?" she asked.

"I don't know," William said. His voice was filled with awe.

"What could be inside?" she said.

"I don't want to find out," William said. His eyes scanned the containers and stopped at one of them. "I just want to find the one with my grandfather in it and get him out."

He walked over to container number seven and wiped the dust off a small instrument panel.

"Minus a hundred and ninety-six Celsius," he read.

"What does this mean?" Iscia asked, pointing to the control panel on one of the other containers. A red light was blinking ominously. William walked over to her.

"This one is at minus ninety-eight. And it's getting warmer," he said, looking at Iscia with concern. "That's the wrong container. And it looks like it's thawing."

He looked at the display again: minus fifty-eight degrees. They could hear rumbling and gurgling inside the container.

"This one's also rising." Iscia pointed at the meter on another container.

"What's going on?" William gasped.

"They're all thawing," Iscia said with dread in her voice. "There's no way this is safe." She took a couple of steps back.

"Depends on what's inside. Maybe the explosion triggered it," William said. They stood there staring at the temperature gauges, which were rapidly rising.

"It's happening to all of them," Iscia said.

Then the meter hit the zero mark on the first tank. Suddenly everything went quiet, and then the container split in two. Gray frost smoke poured out. William and Iscia pulled back as they watched the cold clouds billow toward them like a sleepy flood wave.

"I have a bad feeling about this," Iscia said.

So did William. He raised a trembling hand and pointed

at something moving in front of them—something moving inside the smoke. Something big.

"RUN!" yelled William, yanking Iscia along behind him.

They jumped through the hole in the wall, heading for the tank they had used to blow open the door.

The wall behind them exploded into a cloud of dust and bits of rubble and concrete.

An enormous robot stopped and looked around. Mounted on the top of the body was the head of a wild boar with glowing red eyes and long tusks. The boar bot was as tall as a house. When it spotted William and Iscia, who had reached the tank, it emitted a deafening howl and stomped toward them, causing the floor to shake.

"It's all over," William whispered.

"Look there!" Iscia cried, pointing at something.

William spotted the little beetle. It darted past them and kept going toward the boar bot, which stopped abruptly when it spotted the beetle.

The beetle suddenly started vibrating intensely.

"What is it doing?" Iscia asked, scared.

"No idea," said William.

The boar bot also stood there staring at the tiny beetle, which was now vibrating so violently it seemed to have trouble running. A series of loud clicks came from the beetle as it continued toward the boar.

William froze.

He thought he had heard those clicks before.

But where?

Then the beetle started unfolding. Metal plate upon metal plate seemed to appear from within the beetle. And it kept growing bigger.

"It's shape-shifting," Iscia whispered.

William just stood there, transfixed, staring at the little beetle's dramatic transformation.

The robotic boar took a step back as it stared at the thing that was heading toward it. It was no longer a beetle; for every click and every mechanical change, it became more and more humanoid. It now looked like a huge robot with the head of a beetle. Long metal antennae pierced the air as it picked up speed and headed straight toward the boar.

"It's going to attack the boar," William said. The ground under his feet vibrated for every step the enormous ex-beetle took. The clicking became louder as the beetle robot picked up speed.

The boar bot pulled back and picked up one of the tanks that was beside it. It flung it at the now-enormous beetle-headed robot, which batted the tank away as if it weighed no more than a soccer ball. The beetle bot then stretched out its leg and tripped the boar bot, which hit the ground with a devastating bang. The robot beetle stopped. The dry clicking slowed down.

Click . . . click . . . click . . .

"It saved us!" Iscia cheered.

But William wasn't cheering. He knew now where he had heard that clicking before.

"What is it?" Iscia asked when she saw William's expression. The robot beetle turned around and looked at them.

"I don't think it's over," William whispered, backing up. "That's the one."

"What one?" Iscia asked.

"Abraham's robot. The beetle is the robot," William whispered, crawling up onto the tank. He held his hand out to Iscia and pulled her up after him.

"What robot?" Iscia said.

"The one that attacked us at home in Norway," William whispered.

The hatch in the roof of the tank was still ajar. The robot beetle started toward them. It was bounding across the hall in long strides, flinging aside military trucks and tanks like they were made of paper.

William grabbed the hatch with both hands and pulled with all his strength. The hatch swung open, and William grabbed Iscia's arm and pulled her toward him.

"GET IN!" William shouted. "IT'S NOT GOING TO STOP!"

Iscia jumped through the hatch.

William was right behind her and just managed to shut

the hatch before the robot beetle hit the tank with so much force that it lifted the vehicle right off the ground. Iscia screamed and flailed around for something to hold on to. They crashed to the floor and lay there.

William's ears were ringing. He'd hit his head hard in the collision. He sat up and looked out the window and saw the robot beetle coming back toward them.

"It's coming in for another attack!" he cried, clinging to the seat.

The tank was lifted up. It crashed into a wall and then hit the floor with a loud clang.

"Iscia?" William called out, looking around.

He spotted her underneath one of the seats. He crawled over and shook her. "Iscia? Iscia!" he cried, cautiously rolling her over onto her back.

She didn't respond.

Then the tank was lifted again. William flung himself over Iscia to protect her from the new assault, but it didn't come. William opened his eyes and looked around. He jumped when he saw two glowing eyes peering in at him through one of the windows.

William crawled over to the other window and peered out. The tank was swaying in the robot beetle's hand high above the floor. William knew they wouldn't survive another smashing. He had to do something.

He grabbed the control lever and turned it to the side. The

tank's turret spun around until it was pointed right at the big robot body. Then he felt the tank jerk as it was hoisted even higher. The robot was getting ready to throw them again. William clung to the control panel and hit the fire button. A loud boom echoed around the room. The robot beetle staggered back and forth then fell over backward. The tank dropped to the floor, and everything got quiet.

William lay there, listening. He couldn't hear anything. He crawled over to the window and cautiously looked out. He couldn't see anything.

"Iscia!" William called, coming over to her.

He leaned forward and put his ear to her lips. Was she breathing? "Iscia, can you hear me?"

No reaction.

"ISCIA!"

39

"I think my leg is broken," Iscia moaned.

She was lying on the ground next to one of the submarines. William had found an old mattress and placed his folded jacket under her head.

The robot beetle lay lifeless a short distance away with the tank on top of it.

"Are there more of them coming?" Iscia asked, peering at the robot.

"I don't know," William said. "I've only seen one beetle. I think."

"What about that thing?" Iscia said, pointing at what was left of the boar robot.

"Might be more of them inside the other containers," William said with a shudder.

"Go get your grandfather out of there before any of the others thaw out," Iscia said. "I'll wait here."

"Are you sure?" William asked.

"Yes, I'll yell if I need help," she said, smiling as bravely as she could. "Doesn't sound like any of the other containers are done thawing yet."

"Maybe there was only one of them," William said.

"Let's hope so," Iscia said, and winced in pain. She clutched at her leg.

"I'll be back as soon as I can," William said, and hurried toward the hallway.

William stopped in front of the large containers and checked the displays. The temperatures were still rising—some faster than others. He found container number seven and looked at the temperature meter. The display showed thirty-seven degrees.

He stood there for a few seconds, not knowing what to do. Part of him just wanted to run and get out of there. Who knew what could be in the other containers? But he knew that this was his only chance of seeing his grandfather again, so he stayed.

By the time he noticed an enormous silhouette emerging from one of the other containers, it was already too late. He looked up just in time to see a robot looming over him. A large metallic hand hit him, and then everything went black.

★ ★ ★

What's going on? Where am I?

William sat up cautiously.

His head felt like it was about to explode, and he was wet and cold.

"William?" a voice said. "William, you have to wake up."

"Grandpa?"

William blinked. He could make out a figure in front of him.

"Careful," the voice said. "You suffered a bit of a bump."

William put his hands to his head. "Grandpa?" he repeated.

"Here, give me your hand."

William raised his arm. He felt someone take his hand and help him up to a sitting position.

"There, like that. Very good, now lean back carefully."

William leaned back and felt his back touch the wall behind him. He could make out more details. Two friendly eyes, shaggy gray hair, and a beard.

"Grandpa?"

"Yes, it's me," his grandfather said.

Before William knew it, his arms were draped around his grandfather's neck, hugging him. William's whole body ached, but he didn't care about that. He'd finally found him. He'd found his grandfather!

William jumped when he spotted a gigantic robot looming over him. This one was even bigger than the first. And instead of a boar's head, there was the head of a rhino crowning the huge metal body. The robot stood completely still, staring at him with cold eyes, one hand ready to strike. This one looked even more threatening than the one that had followed them out into the hall.

"Relax. It's deactivated," his grandfather said.

"Deactivated?"

"They have an off button."

"An off button," William repeated. He looked at the other containers.

"Lucky that I thawed out before the rest of them. I froze

them again," his grandfather said, patting the sides of container seven.

They turned around because they heard a deep rumbling from the hall.

William recognized the sound right away. It was the big door. Someone had opened it.

"Is there anyone else in here?" Grandfather practically yelled now.

"Iscia," William said.

"Iscia?" Grandfather repeated.

"Yes, a girl I know from the Institute," William said.

"You brought someone from the Institute down here?" his grandfather exclaimed. He sounded almost angry.

"Yes, she helped me," William said.

His grandfather stormed over to the hole that William had blown in the wall.

"Wait," yelled William, staggering after his grandfather on unsteady legs. "She's on our side."

"I don't believe that," his grandfather said, and pointed to the gigantic door at the other end of the hall. It was slowly opening.

A figure stood at the end of the hallway, waiting. It was Iscia. William gasped. What was she doing?

"Come on," his grandfather yelled, pulling William along behind him.

"But," William said, resisting him. However, his grandfather was a lot stronger than he looked.

"We don't have much time. Come on!" he said, heading for a control panel next to a hatch at the other end of the room. "We have to get you out of here before they come through."

His grandfather hurried over to the robotic boar. He pushed some buttons on its back and took a couple of steps back. William recoiled. The head jerked as the robotic boar opened its eyes and looked around. It spotted William's grandfather and grunted.

"Out there," Grandfather said, pointing toward the hall with all the vehicles. "Get them."

"No! Wait! Iscia!" William yelled.

But Grandfather wasn't listening. The robotic boar howled and stomped out into the hall.

"It should be able to hold them back for a little while," Grandfather said.

He walked over to the control panel again and pushed some buttons. The walls around them started gurgling.

"What's going on?" William cried.

"This is one of the safest bunkers in the world," Grandfather said. "Soon the whole hall out there will fill with water and they won't be able to get us."

William couldn't believe it. Had his grandfather lost his mind? Or had he always been this crazy? It struck William that he didn't actually know his grandfather. He might as well be in here with any random stranger.

"We have to get this open," Grandfather said, walking toward another door at the far side of the room.

"Is that an exit?" William asked.

"No, a way deeper into the system." Suddenly they heard a sound close behind them.

"They're getting nearer," Grandfather mumbled, pulling something out of his inner jacket pocket that looked like a pistol. He aimed it at the door in front of them. A ball of blue light the size of a tennis ball pulverized the door and the wall around it. A thick cloud of dust filled the room.

"Grandpa?" William yelled.

"Come on!" his grandfather answered from somewhere inside the cloud of dust.

William pulled his jacket lapel up over his nose, fumbled his way forward to the hole in the wall, and stopped. There was a tremendous explosion.

The pressure wave was so great that it hurled William through the hole into the darkness.

William landed hard. He stayed on his back for a couple of seconds, trying to catch his breath. But the dust made it hard to breathe.

"Over here," he heard Grandfather say.

William turned over and got up. But it was too dark to see anything.

"Where are we?" he asked.

"We have to get to safety farther down," Grandfather said from the dark. "It's going to take them a little while to get past the boar bot. Follow my voice."

William started walking. He jumped as he felt a hand on his wrist. He tried to pry loose, but the hand was too strong.

"Relax," Grandfather said. "It's only me. Come."

William had no choice but to go where his grandfather led him. Somewhere behind them, William could hear the boar roaring.

They walked through the dark for a while until William's grandfather finally came to a halt.

"This is it," William heard his grandfather say, followed by a loud clack that echoed all around them.

Enormous lamps blinked to life above and revealed something incredible.

William stared in astonishment at the sight before him. They were on an old iron scaffold that was attached to the wall of a gigantic grotto; large amounts of water were pouring out of several holes in the wall.

"This is . . . ," he began, but was interrupted by a deep rumble from the darkness behind them.

"They're in. Hurry." His grandfather pulled him down the rusty, swaying metal staircase, toward the bottom of the grotto.

"Faster," his grandfather yelled.

As soon as they reached the bottom, his grandfather turned around and gave the brittle staircase a vigorous kick.

The stairs shook, came loose from the rock wall, and plunged to the ground.

"How are we going to get back up?" William asked, looking at the rising water. It was up to his knees now.

"We're not going back up again."

"What?" William said.

But his grandfather didn't answer. Instead, his grip tightened round William's wrist.

"WILLIAM!" someone yelled from above.

William glanced up and spotted Fritz Goffman leaning over the railing on the scaffolding way above them.

"Run! Get away!" Goffman yelled. "He's not—"

"Don't listen to him, William," his grandfather said. "It's too late now, anyway."

William looked up at his grandfather. "What do you mean?"

His grandfather didn't respond. He stopped, turned, and stared at William. There was something menacing in the way he looked, as if something had come over him. Something dark. William began to panic. The grip round his wrist grew tighter. It felt like his hand was going to explode.

"You're not my grandfather," he said.

The old man sneered. "It took you a while to figure that out. Don't you think I deserve an Oscar?" The old man's face twitched into a crooked smile. He let go of William's wrist.

"Who are you?" William asked.

"You have no idea how much I've longed for this," he said.

"Abraham?" William whispered. He felt a chill run down his spine.

"Get away, William!" Goffman yelled. "RUN!"

"But . . ." William stared at the old man in front of him. It was as if he was transforming right before William's eyes, as if he was aging even more. His skin was changing color. Now it was almost totally white.

"Your grandfather was wise to freeze me. Extreme cold is the kryptonite of luridium. But he didn't plan on me thawing sooner than him," Abraham said. "And he certainly didn't plan on you being the first one in."

"You're full of luridium." William stared at the old man. He couldn't help but be fascinated.

"That's right," snarled Abraham. "And now I need some more." He looked at William and came closer.

"RUN, WILLIAM!" he heard Iscia scream, but he couldn't move. There was something about the look Abraham was giving him . . . it was as if his whole body had turned into ice.

"Where is my grandfather?" William asked.

"He's up there in number eight. On his way back to dreamland," Abraham said.

"But why did he freeze himself?" William whispered. He had to know.

"He tricked me down here," Abraham continued. "Said he'd give me the luridium that he'd stolen from the Institute."

"Why would he give you more?" William said.

"Why do you think?" Abraham said.

William shook his head. His thoughts felt like syrup.

"To prevent me from getting to you," said Abraham. "He did it to save you. Tricked me down here, locked the gates and froze us both. He really fooled me. But he didn't count on you coming to save him."

"The hologram!" The words just fell out of William's mouth. "It was fake."

"Of course." Abraham smiled. "I still have allies out there. In high places."

Abraham came even closer, staring at William with his cold eyes. "Do you know how you actually get luridium out of a person's body?" he continued, his voice vibrating in anticipation.

William gulped and took a few steps back. The water had reached his pelvis now, and the strong currents were making it difficult for him to stand.

"When the body dies, the luridium's first instinct is to find a new host. So it leaves the body. Choking works best,"

Abraham said, and raised two sinewy hands. "All I need to do is . . . not let go. And the luridium will find me."

"GET AWAY FROM HIM!" he heard Iscia yell. And this time his body obeyed. On sheer instinct, William turned around and started working his way through the water.

"It won't do any good!" he heard Abraham yell after him.

It wasn't easy to get up to speed, the water was up to his waist now. But William clenched his teeth and kept going. He didn't plan to give in without a fight. Not even against Abraham Talley.

William quickly glanced up and saw that Iscia and the others were still standing up there.

He was struggling frantically to keep himself above water. Then he saw a ledge sticking up out of the water ahead of him. He scrambled up onto the little islet and lay there, gasping for breath. His body was completely drained of strength.

"William!" Abraham called.

William rolled over and found himself staring right up at Abraham, who had now taken his true form. His skin hung in folds from his face. His head was hairless, and his cold eyes flashed. It looked like Abraham was finally going to get what he'd been waiting for. The luridium that Grandfather had stolen to save his only grandchild, and the luridium that Abraham needed to keep himself alive.

Abraham took a step toward William and planted one

foot heavily on his stomach. It was hard for William to breathe.

"Please," he begged, but to no avail.

There was nothing William could do as Abraham leaned over him and placed his bony fingers around William's neck and tightened his grip. Despite his ancient body, Abraham was incredibly strong.

William felt his strength ebbing away. But then a memory popped into his head: the vine that had almost strangled him, and the orb that he had used to beat himself free.

Maybe . . .

William coaxed the orb out of his jacket pocket and jabbed it at Abraham's arms.

"Stupid boy." Abraham grinned. "That's not how those things work." He let go of William's neck with one hand and slapped the orb out of his hand.

The orb clanked onto the hard stone floor and rolled away from them. Abraham's free hand returned to William's neck. The bony fingers slowly tightened, and William could feel himself starting to drift. He looked up. Iscia and Goffman were still standing on the ledge, but the two chauffeurs and Laika were climbing down the wreckage of the crumbled staircase. They wouldn't make it in time. Abraham was already squeezing the life out of him.

William felt himself giving up.

What could he do against a man who was full of luridium? He felt his body go numb and his consciousness start to fade away. The water was moving up the sides of his face now. Soon he would either get choked or drown.

But then he felt something else. Familiar vibrations in his stomach. The luridium. Of course, Abraham wasn't the only one who was filled with luridium! He was too.

William concentrated on the vibrations. They grew stronger, moving up through his spine and out into his arms. Suddenly he felt stronger than ever before. He opened his eyes and looked at Abraham. It was like he could feel it too. There was uncertainty in his eyes now.

"No!" he snarled through his teeth. "You're not allowed. It belongs to me."

William lifted his arms and placed his hands on Abraham's wrists, gripping them hard. He focused on the vibrations coursing through his body. When he did, he could feel his own grip tightening and Abraham's fingers loosening.

"Nooooo," Abraham hissed. He leaned over William with all his weight, and his grip tightened again. It felt like a tug of war between two equally strong teams.

William clenched his teeth and, gathering all of his strength, began pulling on Abraham's hands. Slowly he could feel the grip on his neck relaxing again. The bony fingers were pulling away. Abraham's long fingernails rasped along his skin in a desperate attempt to keep his grip.

The water had reached the top of William's face now and was flowing into his eyes and nose. He closed his mouth but felt the water go into his lungs with every desperate breath he took. In one final burst of willpower he managed to pry Abraham's hands away. He could see Abraham screaming in rage but couldn't hear anything but the sound of the water.

The last thing he saw before his face was fully covered was Laika lunging at Abraham and sinking its deadly teeth into the nape of his neck.

William must have lost consciousness, because when he opened his eyes again, all he could see was the ceiling of the grotto. Someone was carrying him. He saw Iscia and Goffman ahead of him. Then one of the chauffeurs looming over him. He was carrying William in his arms. It didn't seem like they had noticed that he had woken up. William turned his head and saw the other chauffeur with Abraham slung over his shoulder. Was he dead?

"There's no way we're going to get out of here before it floods," Iscia said, her voice trembling.

"We have to try," said Goffman.

William was still dazed and very dizzy. He tried to swallow. His throat was sore from Abraham's grip. He tried to speak, but only a hissing sound came out. The chauffeur carrying him looked down but continued on. William could hear the splashing of water all around him. This was bad. Very bad.

They emerged into the cryogenic chamber and stopped. William looked back from where they had come. The water was completely covering the large cave now. It looked like a huge black lake. Everyone was soaking wet. They must have swam or floated up through the water.

"We have to get Tobias out of there," he heard Goffman say.

"And then what?" Iscia said. "Everything is flooding."

A crazy thought popped into William's head.

"The su—" he began, but was overcome by a violent coughing seizure.

"He's back," Iscia shouted, running over to him. She stuck her face so close he could feel her breath on his skin and smiled. "You're back," she said.

"The sub . . . ," William tried again.

"What's he saying?" Goffman said.

"Sub," Iscia said. "What do you mean, William?"

"The subs." William pointed to the hallway outside.

"The submarines," Iscia said, and looked at Goffman. "Do they still work?"

"Only one way to find out," Goffman said. "Which tank is Tobias in?"

"Eight," said William. He could feel himself slipping away again.

"Pry the tank loose," William heard Goffman say. "We have to take the whole thing with us."

William tried to stay conscious as Iscia and Goffman carried him out of the cryogenic chamber and into the enormous hall with all the tanks and submarines. Abraham was strapped onto the back of Laika. The two chauffeurs struggled with the large cryogenic container. It must have weighed more than a car because even they were having a hard time. Now the water had reached the hall, and as the small group came to a halt next to the nearest submarine, it was already up to their knees. The front half of the sub was hidden inside a large tunnel-like hole in the wall.

"Is that the only way in?" Iscia asked, looking up at the hatch that was barely visible on top of the sub.

"Yes," said Goffman.

"How do we get the container up there?" she said. "And us . . ."

"Put me down," said William. The dizziness was gone, and he felt stronger now.

Iscia and Goffman carefully helped William onto his feet. The water felt cool and refreshing. William looked at the cryogenic container.

"Does it float?" he said. The water was rising fast and was already at his waist.

"It's sealed tight," said Goffman. "To keep the liquid nitrogen inside. So yes, it'll float."

"Then we could use the rising water to get it up there," William said.

"Of course!" Goffman shouted, and clapped his hands. "We might have a chance after all."

Moments later they had reached the top of the enormous submarine. The two chauffeurs climbed on top of the sub and started turning the large wheel on the outside of the hatch.

"Quickly," Goffman shouted. "We have to get inside before the water reaches the top."

There was a muffled clank inside the door, and the chauffeurs forced the old hatch up.

"NOW . . . everyone help," Goffman shouted, and started pulling on the cryogenic container.

As the water reached the open hatch, it started to stream into the sub, and the cryogenic container was sucked in through the hatch and clanked onto the metal floor below. The rest of the group followed. William was the last one in. He grabbed the hatch and tried to force it shut. But the stream of water was so strong now, it seemed an impossible task. The two chauffeurs came to his rescue, and together they managed to seal it.

Soon the small group had gathered inside the large control room.

"Now what?" Goffman shouted.

"What about that one?" William said, and pointed at two large red levers marked EJECT.

"Do it!" Goffman commanded.

William flicked both levers at once and pulled back. They stood for a while, waiting. But nothing happened.

"Do it again!" said Goffman. His voice was trembling now.

William pulled the levers one more time. This time a deep rumble made the whole sub shake.

"That's probably the motors," William whispered.

"Let's hope so," Iscia said as she scanned the surroundings with wary eyes.

The rumble grew louder. The sub shook and roared like a space shuttle before it suddenly shot forward and everyone fell to the floor.

William's arms waved frantically in the air as he tried to grab hold of something.

Anything.

But there was nothing to hang on to, so he tumbled backward and slammed into the wall of the submarine.

There was a loud swishing all around. It sounded like water rushing past outside the metal hull. Then it felt like the gigantic sub suddenly turned its nose downward and went into a dive.

William suddenly floated up in the air before slamming onto the floor. He slid forward and caught a glimpse of Iscia, who was holding on to a hatch in the wall.

"Iscia!" William shouted as he continued past her and crashed into a metal cabinet.

"GRAB HOLD OF SOMETHING!" Goffman's voice shouted from somewhere in the chaos.

Then it seemed like the whole sub tipped backward and shot upward.

William's fingers scraped desperately at the cabin in a vain attempt to keep from sliding backward again. But it was no use. As the front of the sub shot up, William and the others tumbled backward and landed in a heap of arms and legs at the end of the control room.

The sound of the water rushing past on the outside was so loud now it was no use trying to talk.

So William closed his eyes.

And for a moment he thought that this was it.

The end.

Then everything went quiet.

He raised his head in surprise and looked at Iscia, who was squashed up against the wall behind him.

"We've stopped," he said.

"You sure?" Iscia asked.

"Think so." William got to his feet and staggered toward the hatch in the ceiling. Suddenly he had to get out. Had to get fresh air. If there was any out there.

He grabbed the hatch. He must have been full of adrenaline, and much stronger than he would have been under normal circumstances, because the wheel turned easily. He pushed the hatch open.

Bright sunlight and fresh air shot down at him. He squinted as he climbed onto the deck of the sub and took a deep breath.

There was a frantic flashing of bright lights from somewhere near by. Excited voices talking.

He rubbed his eyes and blinked. There was a boat in front of him, filled with people. They all had cameras, and they were taking pictures of him. There was something written on the side of the boat: THAMES TOURS.

He looked around. There was Big Ben and the Tower of London. . . . The sub was floating in the middle of the River Thames.

And that's when he felt it again. The pain in his throat where Abraham had tried to choke him. He felt dizzy, and his legs seemed to disappear from under him.

He fell.

41

William opened his eyes.

He was lying in a hospital bed with a lot of wires hooked up to his body and to machines positioned around the bed.

He could hear the sound of a monitor beeping every time his heart beat. A clear bag with some kind of liquid in it was hanging from a stand next to the bed. A tube ran from the bag into the back of his hand. He tried to swallow. It hurt. He needed some water.

Now that his eyes had adjusted to the light, he could see more of the room. He wasn't alone.

Someone was standing over by the window. He couldn't see who it was. The sunlight was too bright.

"Thirsty . . . ," he said. His voice was hoarse, and it hurt to talk. He coughed a couple of times.

The person turned around and looked at him. "William, you're awake!"

Iscia? William thought.

She came over to him to stand next to the bed, looking down at him and smiling. "You've been in an induced coma for a week," she said. "How are you feeling?"

"Thirsty," William repeated, and started coughing again.

"Of course," Iscia said, and hurried over to a sink in the corner.

She came back to the bed with a cup. William lifted his head off the pillow and drank.

"My head is killing me," he said, and put his fingers to his forehead. Iscia pulled a red cord that was hanging on the wall.

"Where am I?" William asked.

"At the Institute," Iscia said.

"I'm not dead?"

"No, but it was close." Iscia grew serious. "Abraham almost managed to get the luridium out of your body."

"The luridium," William repeated. Everything seemed like a distant nightmare now. "So you know that I have luridium in my body . . . ?"

"Yes, I know," she said, and smiled. "But you're not like the other machines. Even if you are forty-nine percent less human than I thought."

William had to smile. He didn't really know why, but it was nice to hear Iscia say that. They looked at each other for a moment.

Things started coming back to him now.

The sub.

The River Thames.

"The sub," he said. "It worked."

Iscia smiled. "If it hadn't been for your idea about the sub, we'd probably still be down there."

"What about my grandfather?" William asked. Iscia grew somber.

"Your grandfather is in the isolation ward. They say there's a chance he'll wake up."

"A chance?" William repeated. "So there's a chance that he might not then too?"

Iscia looked down. "You'll have to talk to the others," she said briefly.

"I have to see him." William tried to get up but collapsed back onto the bed.

"What about Abraham?" he asked.

"He's on ice again in an escape-proof container somewhere here at the Institute. I don't think we'll be seeing any more of him," Iscia said. "I don't know that much about it, but Goffman said that the luridium Abraham has in his body has been in there so long it absorbed the last of what made him human."

William shrugged. He didn't like the thought of Abraham being at the Institute, but at least they knew where he was now. *And* they could control him.

Iscia hesitated a little. "There's something I have to tell you," she said finally.

"What?"

"You know my folder? The one I found in the Archive? There was a reason I didn't want to tell you what was in it, what my job was," she said.

"Why? What was your job?" William asked.

"It was you," she said after a pause.

"Me?" William asked.

"Yeah," Iscia said. "My job was to keep an eye on you in case anything happened. And boy did something happen!"

William lay there staring at her.

"That's why you found me in London," he said.

"Yeah," she said. "I'm sorry I couldn't tell you the truth. There was too much at stake. Someone had to be with you in the tunnels," she said a little ashamedly.

"I understand." William took her hand.

William didn't know why he'd taken her hand like that. It just happened. They looked at each other for a few seconds without saying anything. William didn't know what to do now. Should he let go and pretend it hadn't happened, or should he continue holding it. Both ideas seemed too stupid. He smiled awkwardly. Iscia smiled back.

He quickly pulled his hand away as the door opened and Slapperton tumbled into the room. "William," he began after he'd caught his breath. He stood there, opening and closing his mouth like a goldfish, staring at William. "Uh, I, uh . . . ," he tried once more.

Then the door opened again, and Goffman rushed in. He stopped next to Slapperton.

"You're awake," he said.

"Yes," said William.

"I, uh . . . I . . . ," Goffman continued, but had to give up.

"What they're trying to say is that they're really happy to see you again," Iscia said with a smile. "And they're sorry about all of that."

Slapperton and Goffman blushed.

"Right?" Iscia prompted.

"Um, yeah," Slapperton said.

"Yeah," Goffman said.

A few days later William was sitting, buckled in, on the soft sofa in the Institute's big plane. His body was trembling. In a couple of hours he would see his parents again at home in Norway.

It seemed like an eternity since he'd seen them, and Mr. Turnbull, and the rest of the class. So much had happened. He felt different.

A sound made him look up.

A figure was approaching from the other end of the cabin. Was it . . . ?

"Relax, it's me this time," the figure said, and smiled.

"Grandpa?" William said hesitantly.

His grandfather sat and studied him for a bit. "You've grown," he said.

William didn't know what to say. "Thank you?"

His grandfather laughed a little. "There's been a bit of improvement since the last time I saw you, in the hospital eight years ago," he said. "And you've become a bit of a code breaker, I understand."

"Mm," William said. "But I think I'm going to take a little break from cryptography now."

His grandfather smiled and scratched his beard. Then he reached his arm behind his back and scratched there, too. "Side effect of being frozen for so long. It'll pass eventually."

They sat for a while just looking at each other.

"It's really good seeing you again," Grandfather said. He smiled, almost shyly.

William just couldn't help himself anymore. He leaped at his grandfather and did something he had dreamed of doing for as long as he could remember. He flung his arms round his grandfather's neck and hugged him.

"I thought I would never see you again," William said.

"Me too," Grandfather said. William could hear that he was holding back tears.

"What will you do now?" William asked.

"Go home with you and say hello to your parents. I owe them an explanation too. And then I'm going to try to convince them to let you come back to the Institute again, if you want." Grandfather pulled away and looked down at William. "Do you?" he asked.

There was nothing in the world that William wanted more than go back to the Institute.

"Yes," he said, and grinned.

42

"BREAKFAST!" William's father yelled from downstairs.

William was bent over his desk, working. He was looking through a big magnifying glass as he tightened a tiny screw into something that looked like a little mechanical beetle.

Then it was his mother's turn. "BREAKFAST!" she hollered.

"Coming!" William replied, and set down his screwdriver.

He set the beetle on the desk, looked at it, and smiled. It didn't look that much like the other beetle, but close enough. William hadn't gotten it to move yet. But he had plenty of time.

"WILLIAM!" his father yelled.

He got up, grabbed his school backpack, and ran out of the room.

Down in the kitchen everything was like it had been

before, minus all the books. Now there was room to move around. His mom and dad were sitting at the kitchen table.

"Pancakes," his mom said with a smile. "Even if you're only fifty-one percent human, you still need breakfast."

"Oh, leave the kid alone," his dad said.

"Are you looking forward to going back to school again?" his mom asked.

"Not that much," William said, rolling up his pancake. He raised it to his mouth and was about to take a bite of it when a car horn honked outside.

"That must be him. He insisted on driving you to school. You'll just have to eat it in the car," his mom said. "Good luck!"

A shiny white car was parked out front.

The door opened automatically, and William hopped in.

"Pancake?" his grandfather said, eyeing the breakfast William was holding rolled up in his hand. "I love pancakes."

"You want it?" William asked.

"No thanks, I just ate."

William cast a glance at the two chauffeurs in the front seat. He still didn't like them. One of them scowled at him in the rearview mirror.

The car started moving.

"Well, how does it feel?" his grandfather asked, looking at William.

"How does what feel?" William asked.

"Not having to live in secrecy anymore?"

"It feels good," William said.

"Excellent," his grandfather said.

"Did you have a chance to talk to Mom and Dad about the Institute?" William asked, slightly nervously.

"Yes?" his grandfather said, and smiled. "They still need a little more convincing, but it's going to work out. I'll make sure it does."

They sat there in silence for a bit.

"But you won't be seeing me for a while," his grandfather said eventually.

"Why not?" William asked. It felt like a blow to his gut.

"I'm going on a little trip."

"Where to?"

"Tibet."

"Tibet!" William exclaimed. "What are you going to do there?"

"Get something," his grandfather said with a sly smile.

"How long are you going to be there?" William asked.

"I'm not sure. A few weeks, maybe more. We'll see." His grandfather smiled. "I'm really proud of you, William."

"Thanks," William said.

"I think we're here," his grandfather said as the car pulled up outside the school. William's door swung open.

"You'd better hurry. It looks like the bell already rang," his grandfather said.

William just stood there outside the car.

"Was there something else, William?" his grandfather asked.

"There's something I've been doing a little thinking about." William hesitated.

"Yes?"

"If no one could get into that bunker, why was it full of submarines and tanks from the Second World War?"

"A very good question, William," his grandfather said with a knowing smile. "Someday I'll tell you. But for now you have to forget all that and concentrate on school, at least for a little while. Okay?"

"Okay," William said, and closed the door.

He waved and started jogging toward the door to the school. The white Rolls Royce disappeared around a corner.

Everyone looked at William when he walked into the classroom. He stopped when he saw Mr. Turnbull, who was standing at the board with a small eraser in his hand. Mr. Turnbull stood there for a long time, staring at him. It seemed like he was trying to find the right words.

"So, your last name is Wenton now?" he finally said. "William Wenton?"

"Yes," said William. "It is."

About the Author

Bobbie Peers is a graduate of the London International Film School. He made his mark on Norwegian film history in 2006 when he won a Palme d'Or for his film *Sniffer*, which he wrote and directed. In 2015 Peers made his debut as a children's books author. *William Wenton and the Impossible Puzzle* (original title: *William Wenton and the Luridium Thief*) is the first book in a forthcoming series featuring the code-breaking whiz William.